OUTBACK
HEIRESS,
SURPRISE
PROPOSAL

OUTBACK HEIRESS, SURPRISE PROPOSAL

BY

MARGARET WAY

First published in Great Britain 2009
Large Print edition 2009
Harlequin Mills & Boon Limited,
Eton House, 18-24 Paradise Road,
Richmond, Surrey TW9 1SR

© Margaret Way Pty., Ltd. 2009

ISBN: 978 0 263 20630 2

Set in Times Roman 16 on 18¼ pt.
16-1009-55991

Harlequin Mills & Boon policy is to use papers that are
natural, renewable and recyclable products and made
from wood grown in sustainable forests. The logging and
manufacturing process conform to the legal environmental
regulations of the country of origin.

Printed and bound in Great Britain
by CPI Antony Rowe, Chippenham, Wiltshire

PROLOGUE

IT HAPPENED very unexpectedly—as an extraordinary number of things tend to do. An unusually tense meeting of the board of the giant mining company Titan was in progress. Sir Francis Forsyth, Chairman and CEO of the company, and patriarch of the largest land-owning family in the country, was seen to be becoming increasingly angered by some concerns being voiced by his middle-aged son and heir, Charles.

The still strikingly handsome septuagenarian, piercing blue eyes narrowed, addressed his hapless son in a tone of voice that sent a shiver of pity through the other board members who found this belittling of Charles very much like a public caning. The general feeling was that Charles, admittedly not the brightest chip off the block, endured a lot of punishment from his dynamo of a father, who looked on him with a ferocious disappointment he rarely bothered to hide.

Like now.

'Charles, when are you going to face the fact you're becoming a bloody liability around here?' Sir Francis gritted, removing his glasses. 'Because that's what you are. You are not the man to find solutions to problems. You have to look to *me* as your source of guidance. Not fire off these pie-in-the-sky suggestions. You do realise as a business-man *profit* is the name of the game? That and keeping our shareholders happy. Yet you continue to—' He broke off abruptly as another voice, vibrantly attractive, completely self-assured, spoke up in defence of the now ashen-faced Charles.

'What is it, Bryn?' Sir Francis turned his handsome head with exaggerated patience to the young man on his right.

Bryn Macallan was the brilliant grandson of his late partner, Sir Theodore Macallan, co-founder of Titan. Everyone on the board shared that opinion. Sir Francis, too, greatly admired him, yet para-doxically also feared him. Bryn Macallan, who had already gained an impressive reputation at an early age, was the real thing. An actual chip off the old block. On top of everything else, he was making it increasingly difficult for Sir Francis to retain the control he had settled into since Theo had died some years back. Bryn Macallan, no bones about it, was after the top job sooner rather than later—and there didn't seem a damned thing Francis Forsyth could do about it.

Could it perhaps be divine retribution?

'I'm drawn to at least some of Charles's suggestions,' Bryn was saying, completely unfazed by the chairman's mood and attitude. 'We *do* have a duty of care to our workers. We have the expert's safety report on Mount Garnet. We've all had time to read it.' He glanced around the table to receive confirmation. 'I'd like to raise a few concerns of my own, as well as making some additional suggestions as to how we can best go about implementing necessary changes. We have the eyes of the nation on us. We carry a great responsibility. I know we're all aware of that.'

'Hear, hear!' Several of the other board members—the most powerful and influential, it had to be noted—nodded.

Bryn Macallan, though barely thirty, was held in very high regard around the table. The way he looked, the way he spoke, and his formidable brain power brought vividly to mind his late, deeply lamented grandfather. Bryn Macallan was the up-and-coming man. He far outstripped poor

Charles, or indeed any other contender for the top job. Such was his aura. An aura given to few people.

Francis Forsyth more than anyone else was acutely aware of it. 'We are indeed, Bryn,' he countered smoothly, knowing Bryn's recommendations would be positive, but less harmful to Titan. He needed to be heeded. 'I'm equally sure we're all eager to listen to what you have to say. But not to Charles's blathering. He sounds like a man on some sort of guilt trip.'

Charles sat frozen in place. 'Why do you do this to me, Dad?' he asked with a bizarrely child-like hurt in his voice. 'Never a word of encouragement.'

Maddened, Sir Francis jabbed the air with a forceful finger. It made not only his son flinch. 'The last thing *you* need is encouragement,' he told his heir blisteringly. 'You can't seem to understand—' He stopped to draw more breath into his lungs. The breath appeared to fail. Instead, it turned into a violent paroxysm of coughing.

Bryn Macallan, predictably, was the first to react.

'Get the paramedics here *now!*' he shouted, rising swiftly from his chair. He was sure all at once that this was something very serious. Alarmingly so. But before he could get to Sir

Francis, the chairman slumped sideways, then toppled to the floor, his face taking on the colour of a wax sculpture.

The life of arguably the richest and certainly one of the most powerful men in the country was all but over.

Bryn began CPR—he had to if there was any chance of saving Sir Francis. He was thankful he had spent time perfecting the procedure.

The paramedics, urgently despatched, arrived in under six minutes. They took over from Bryn Macallan, but it was evident to them all that the nation's 'Iron Man' was dead.

Charles Forsyth was so shocked by the violence and suddenness of the event he sat in the grip of paralysis, unable to stand, let alone speak. The truth was he had thought his father was going to live for ever.

It was left to Bryn Macallan to take charge. Bryn, though he experienced the collective shock, felt no great grief. Sir Frank Forsyth had lived and died a ruthless man—brilliant, but guilty of many sins. Wearing the deep camouflage of long friendship he had done terrible things to the Macallan family in business since the death of his grandfather.

'Frank has always had the potential to be an out-and-out scoundrel,' Bryn's grandmother had warned him after his grandfather's funeral. 'It was Theo, as honourable a man as Frank is amoral, who kept that potential for ruthlessness in check. Now Frank holds the reins. Mark my words, Bryn, darling. It's time now for the Macallans to look out!'

Her prediction had been spot-on. Since then bitter rivalries and deep resentments had run like subterranean rivers through everything the Forsyths and the Macallans did. But the two families were tied together through Titan.

The Forsyths had their vision. Bryn Macallan had his.

It was Frank Forsyth and Theo Macallan, geologists, friends through university, who had started up Titan in the late 1960s. They had discovered, along with part-aboriginal tracker Gulla Nolan, a fabulous iron-ore deposit at Mount Gloriana, in the remote North-West of the vast state of Western Australia—a state which took up one-third of the huge island continent. Today this company, Titan, was a mighty colossus.

Within minutes the death of the nation's 'Iron

Man' was part of breaking news on television, radio and the internet. The extended family was informed immediately. The only family member not present in the state capital, Perth, was Francesca Forsyth. She was the daughter of Sir Frank's second son, Lionel, who had been killed along with his wife and their pilot in a light plane crash en route from Darwin to Alice Springs. Francesca had been orphaned at age five.

It had been left to her uncle Charles and his wife Elizabeth to take on the job of raising her. Indeed, Elizabeth had taken the bereaved little girl to her heart, although she and Charles had a daughter of their own—Carina, their only child, some three years older than her cousin. Carina had grown up to be the acknowledged Forsyth heiress; Francesca who shunned the limelight was 'the spare'.

What was not known by society and the general public alike was that Carina Forsyth, for most of her privileged life, had harboured a deep, irrational jealousy of her young cousin—though she did her best to hide it. Over the years she had almost perfected the blurring of the boundaries between her true nature and the role of older, wiser cousin she presented to the world. But sadly

Carina was on a quest to destroy any chance of happiness her cousin might have in life. She had convinced herself from childhood that Francesca had stolen her mother's love. And the melancholy truth was that, although Elizabeth Forsyth loved her daughter, and went to great lengths to demonstrate it, the beautiful little girl, 'child of light' Francesca, through the sweetness of her nature *had* gained a large portion of her aunt's heart.

Francesca, acutely intelligent and possessed of a sensitive, intuitive nature, had not been unaware of her cousin's largely hidden malevolence. Consequently she had learned very early not to draw her cousin's fire, and was equally careful not to attract undue attention. *Carina Forsyth* was the Forsyth heiress. What Carina did not appreciate was that Francesca had never found any difficulty with that. Enormous wealth could be a great blessing or a curse, depending on one's point of view. Being an heiress was not part of Francesca's ethos.

Even the cousins' looks were polarised. Both young women were beautiful. Not just an accolade bestowed on them by a fawning press. A simple statement of fact. Carina was a stunner: tall, curvy, a blue-eyed blonde with skin like thick cream, and supremely self-assured as only those *born* rich could be. Francesca, by contrast, was raven-haired, olive-skinned, and with eyes that were neither grey nor green but took colour from what she was wearing. Seen together at the big functions their grandfather had expected both young women to attend, they made startling foils: one so golden, secure in her own perfection, with the eye-catching presence of—some said cattishly behind her back—a showgirl, and the other with an air of refinement that held more than a touch of mystery. Carina went all out to play up her numerous physical assets. Francesca had chosen to downplay her beauty, for obvious reasons.

The greatest potential for danger lay in the fact that both young women were in love with the same man. Bryn Macallan. Carina's feelings for him were very much on show. Indeed, she treated Bryn with astonishing possessiveness, managing to convey to all that a deep intimacy existed between them. Francesca had always been devastated by the knowledge. Indeed, she had to live with constant heartache. Bryn preferred Carina to her. There was nothing else to do but accept it—even if it involved labouring not to show her true feelings. She knew exactly what might happen if she allowed her emotions to surface, however briefly. There could be only one outcome.

What Carina wanted, Carina got.

While the heiress was at the family mansion to receive the news, Francesca was at Daramba, the flagship of the Forsyth pastoral empire, in Queensland's Channel Country. Francesca, a gifted artist herself, since leaving university— albeit with a first-class law degree—had involved herself in raising the profile of Aboriginal artists and acting as agent and advisor in the sale of their works. For one so young—she was only twenty-three—she had been remarkably successful.

Unlike her glamorous high society cousin, Francesca Forsyth felt the burden of great wealth. She wanted to give back. It was the driving force that paved the way to her strong commitment to the less fortunate in the broad community.

Francesca, it was agreed, needed to be told face to face of her grandfather's sudden death and brought home. Bryn Macallan elected to do it. An experienced pilot, he would fly the corporation's latest Beech King Air. He was considered by everyone to be the best man for the job. Though everyone knew the late Sir Frank had dearly wished for a match between Bryn and his elder granddaughter Carina, the fulfilment of that wish had always eluded him. The two rival families were also keenly aware that Bryn and Francesca shared a special *bond,* which was not to be broken for all the families' tensions. Bryn Macallan was, therefore, the man to bring Francesca home.

CHAPTER ONE

LOOKING down on the ancient Dreamtime land-scape, Bryn experienced such a feeling of elation it lifted the twin burdens of ambition and family responsibility from his shoulders—if only for a time. He loved this place—Daramba. He and his family had visited countless times over the years, when his much-loved grandfather had been alive. These days his mother and his grandmother didn't come. For them the close association had ended on the death of Sir Theo, when Francis Forsyth—mega-maniac, call him what you will—got into full stride. It had been left to Bryn to bridge the gap. It was part of his strategy. His womenfolk knew what he was about. They were one hundred per cent behind him. But in spite of everything—even the way his family had been stripped of so much power by stealth—he found Daramba miraculous.

The name in aboriginal, with the accent on the second syllable, meant waterlily—the native symbol of fertility. One of nature's most exquisite flowers, the waterlily was the totemic Dreamtime ancestor of the Darambal tribe. The vast cattle station, one of the largest in the land of the cattle kings, was set in the Channel Country's riverine desert. That meant it boasted numerous lagoons in which waterlilies abounded. This was the year the long drought had broken over many parts of the Queensland Outback, giving tremendous relief to the Inland. Daramba's countless waterways, which snaked across the station, the secret swamps where the pelicans made their nests, and the beautiful lagoons would be floating a magnificent display. Even so, there was nothing more thrilling than to see the mighty landscape, its fiery red soil contrasting so brilliantly with the opal-blue sky, cloaked by a glorious mantle of wildflowers that shimmered away to the horizon.

It was a breathtaking display, almost too beautiful to bear—as if the gates of heaven had been opened for a short time to man. All those who were privileged to see the uncompromising desert turned into the greatest floral display on earth—and there weren't all that many—even those who knew the desert intimately, still went in awe of this phenomenal rebirth that flowed over the land in a great tide.

Then, when the waters subsided, came the all too brief period of utter magic when the wildflowers had their dazzling days in the sun: the stiff paper daisies, the everlastings that didn't wilt when plucked, white, bright yellow and pink, the crimson Sturt Peas, the Parrot peas, the native hibiscus, the Spider lilies and the Morgan flowers, the poppies and the Firebushes, the pure white Carpet of Snow, the exquisite little cleomes that were tucked away in the hills, the lilac Lambs' Tails and the green Pussy Tails that waved back and forth on the wind. One would have to have a heart of stone not to be moved by such a spectacle.

Bryn was vividly reminded of how in her childhood Francesca had revelled in the time of the flowers. All those miles upon miles of flowers and perfume. It had been her own childhood fantasy, her dreamworld, one of her ways of surviving the tragic loss of her parents. He remembered her as a little girl, running off excitedly into an ocean of white paper daisies, her silvery laughter filling the air, while she set about making a chain of the wildflowers to wear as a diadem atop her long hair. Beautiful hair, with the polished gloss of a magpie's wing. Usually Carina had ruined things, by eventually tugging the garland off her younger cousin's head and throwing it away, claiming the paper daisies might be harbouring bugs. The truth of it was Carina had been sending out a message that demanded to be heard. Francesca was meant to live in her shadow. And she never let her forget it.

'There's no telling where this might end!' his grandmother, Lady Macallan, had once confided, a furrow of worry between her brows. 'Carina deeply resents our little Francey. And it will only grow worse.'

It *had*. Though a lot of people didn't see it, Carina was very cunning—but Francey wouldn't hear a word against her. That was the essential sweetness of her nature. Francey was no fool— Bryn was certain she privately admitted to herself that Carina was as devious and manipulative as that old devil Sir Frank, and he knew he, himself, was a bit of an erotic obsession with Carina. It was naked in her eyes, every time she looked at him. And he had to admit to a brief, hectic affair with her when the two of them were younger. Carina was a beautiful young woman, but, as he had come to discover, there was something twisted in her soul. He supposed he could live with it as long as no harm came to Francey—who, in her way, was as big an obsession with Carina as he was. Carina's mother, Elizabeth, had doted on the angelic bereaved child that had been Francesca. She had taken Francey to her heart. That was when it had all started. He was sure of it.

The Beech King Air B100, their latest acquisition, was flying like a bird. It differed from Titan's other King Airs, its model easy to distinguish on the ground, with different engine exhausts, and the propellers in flat pitch at rest. Bryn loved flying. He found it enormously relaxing. He had already commenced his descent. The roof of the giant hangar was glinting like molten silver, almost dazzling his shielded eyes. He fancied he could smell the scents of the wild bush. There was no other smell like it. Dry, aromatic, redolent of vast open spaces and flower-filled plains.

Station kids on their lunchbreak ran at him the instant he stopped the station Jeep. He patted heads and shoulders while distributing a small hoard of sweets, asking how they were doing and telling a few kid-oriented jokes that were greeted with merry peals of laughter. Rosie Williams, the young schoolteacher, stood on the porch, smiling a bright welcome.

'Good to see you, Mr Macallan.'

'Good to see you too, Rosie.' He sketched a brief salute. No matter how many times he told her to call him Bryn, she couldn't get round to it. 'Hope these kids aren't giving you any trouble?' He ruffled the glossy curls of a little aboriginal child standing next to him, confidently holding his hand.

'No, no—everything's fine. We're making a lot of progress.'

'Great to hear it.'

More giggles. Sunlight falling on glowing young faces.

A few minutes later he was back in the Jeep, waving a friendly hand. He hoped to find Francesca at the homestead, but that was all it was—*hope*. He'd probably have to go looking for her. The remote station had not yet been contacted with news of Sir Frank's death. Best the news came from him. Face to face.

Five minutes more and he came into full view of the homestead. After Frank Forsyth had acquired the valuable property in the late 1970s he'd lost little time knocking down the once proud old colonial mansion that had stood on the spot for well over one hundred years, erecting a huge contemporary structure more in keeping with his tastes. Eventually he'd even got rid of the beautiful old stone fountain that had graced the front court, which had used to send sparks of silver water out onto the paved driveway. Bryn remembered the three wonderful winged horses that had held up the basins.

His grandfather, when he had first seen the new homestead, had breathed, *'Dear God!'*

Bryn remembered it as though it were yesterday. Sir Francis had come tearing out of the house when he'd heard their arrival, shouting a full-throated greeting, demanding to know what his friend thought.

'It's very *you,* Frank,' his grandfather had said.

Even as a boy he had heard the irony Sir Frank had missed.

'Fantastic, Sir Francis!' Bryn had added his own comment weakly, not wanting to offend the great Sir Francis Forsyth, his grandad's lifelong friend and partner. Anyway the new homestead *was* fantastic—like a super-modern research station.

It faced him now. A massive one-storey building of steel, poured concrete and glass, four times as big as the original homestead, its only nod to tradition the broad covered verandahs that surrounded the structure on three sides. No use calling it a house or a home. It was a *structure.* Another monument to Sir Frank. The right kind of landscaping might have helped to soften the severity of the façade, but the approach was kept scrupulously clear. One was obviously entering a New Age Outback homestead.

Jili Dawson, the housekeeper, a strikingly attractive woman in her early fifties, greeted him with a dazzling smile and a light punch in the arm.

'Long time, no see!'

'Been busy, Jili.' He smiled into liquid black eyes that were alight with affection. Jili's eyes clearly showed her aboriginal blood, which came from her mother's side. Her father had been a white stockman, but Jili identified far more with her mother's family. Her skin was completely unlined, a polished amber, and her soft voice carried the familiar lullaby rhythms of her mother's people. 'I don't suppose I'm lucky enough to find Francey at home?' he asked, casting a glance into an entrance hall as big as a car park.

'No way!' Jili gave an open-handed expansive wave that took in the horizon. 'She with the group, paintin' out near Wungulla way. Hasn't bin home for coupla days. She's okay, though. Francey knows her way around. Besides, all our people look after her.'

'Wasn't that always the way, Jili?' he said, thinking how close contact with the tribal people had enriched his own and Francey's childhood. Carina had never been a part of any of that, holding herself aloof. 'Listen, Jili, I've come with serious news. We didn't let you know yesterday because I was coming to fetch Francey and tell her in person.'

'The man's dead.' Jili spoke very calmly, as though the event had already cast its shadow—or as if it was written on his forehead.

'Who told you?' He frowned. 'Did one of the other stations contact you?' News got around, even in the remote Inland. On the other hand Jili had the uncanny occult gift of tribal people in foretelling the future.

Jili rocked back and forth slowly. 'Just knew what you were gunna say before you said it. That was one helluva man. Good and evil. Plagued by devils, but devils of his own makin'. We know that, both of us. I honoured your fine, wise grandad, and your dear dad. A great tragedy when he bin killed in that rock fall. But they're with their ancestors now. They look down from the stars that shine on us at night. I have strong feelings for your family. You bin very kind to me. Treat me right. Lot rests on *your* shoulders, Bryn, now Humpty Dumpty has gone and fallen off the wall. What I want to know is this—is it gunna change things for Jacob and me? Are we gunna lose our jobs?'

Jacob Dawson, Jili's husband, also part aboriginal, was a long-time leading hand on the station—one of the best. In Bryn's opinion Daramba couldn't do without either of them. And Jacob would make a far better overseer than the present one, Roy Forster, who relied far too heavily on Jacob and his diverse skills.

'It all has to be decided, Jili,' he said, with a heartfelt sigh. 'Charles will inherit. I can't speak for him. He can't even speak for himself at the moment. He's in deep shock.'

Jili looked away, unseeing. 'Thought his dad was gunna live for ever,' she grunted. 'Seems he was as human as the rest of us. How have the rest of 'em reacted?' She turned to stare into Bryn's brilliant dark eyes. They were almost as black as her own, yet different because of their diamond glitter.

'Some are in shock,' he said. 'Some are in surprisingly good cheer,' he added dryly.

'Well, wait on the will,' Jili advised. 'See if he try to put things to rights. There's an accounting, ya know.'

Bryn didn't answer. In any case, it was much too late now. His grandfather and his father were gone. He came to stand beside her, both of them looking out at the quicksilver mirage. They both knew it was the end of something. The end of an era, certainly. But the fight was still on.

Jili was watching him. She thought of Bryn Macallan as a prince, grave and beautiful; a prince who acknowledged *all* his subjects. A prince who was ready to come into his rightful inheritance. She laid a gentle, respectful hand on his shoulder. 'I promise you it be right in the end, Bryn. But a warning you must heed. There's a bad spell ahead. Mind Francey. That cousin of hers is just waitin' to swoop like a hawk on a little fairy wren. Bad blood there.'

Wasn't that his own fear?

He changed up a gear as he came on a great sweep of tall grasses that covered the flat, fiery red earth. Their tips were like golden feathers blowing in the wind. It put him in mind of the open savannahs of the tropical North. That was the effect of all the miraculous rain. The four-wheel drive cut its way through the towering grasses like a bulldozer, flattening them and creating a path before they sprang up again, full of sap and resilience. A lone emu ducked away on long grey legs. It had all but been hidden in its luxuriant camouflage as it fed on shoots and seeds. The beautiful ghost gums, regarded by most as the quintessential eucalypt but not a eucalypt at all, stood sentinel to the silky blue sky, glittering grasses at their feet. It was their opal-white boles that made them instantly recognisable.

A string of billabongs lay to his right. He caught the glorious flashy wings of parrots diving in and out of the Red River gums. Australia—the land of parrots! Such a brilliant range of colours: scarlet, turquoise, emerald, violet, an intense orange and a bright yellow. Francey, when six, had nearly drowned in one of those lagoons—the middle one, Koopali. It was the deepest and the longest, with permanent water even in drought. In that year the station had been blessed with good spring rains, so Koopali, which could in flood become a raging monster, had been running a bumper. On that day it had been Carina who had stood by, a terrified witness, unable to move to go to her cousin's assistance, as though all strength had been drained out of her nine-year-old body.

It was a miracle Bryn had come upon them so quickly. Magic was as good an answer as any. A sobbing, inconsolable Carina had told them much later on that they had wandered away from the main group and, despite her warnings, Francey had insisted on getting too close to the deep lagoon. With its heavy load of waterlilies a child could get enmeshed in the root system of all the aquatic plants and be sucked under. Both girls could swim, but Francey at that time had been very vulnerable, being only a beginner and scarcely a year orphaned.

Could she really have disobeyed her older cousin's warnings? Francey as a child had never been known to be naughty.

When it had been realised the two girls had wandered off, the party had split up in a panic. He had never seen people move so fast. Danger went hand in hand with the savage grandeur of the Outback. He had run and run, his heartbeats almost jammed with fear, heading for Koopali. Why had he done that? Because that was where one of the itinerant aboriginal women, frail and of a great age, had pointed with her message stick. He had acted immediately on her mysterious command. Yet how could she have known? She'd been almost blind.

'*Koopali,*' she had muttered, nodding and gesturing, marking the word with an emphatic down beat of her stick.

To this day he didn't know why he had put such trust in her. But he had, arriving in time to launch himself into the dark green waters just as Francey's small head had disappeared for probably the last time. That was when Carina had started screaming blue murder...

So there it was: he had saved Francey's life, which meant to the aboriginal people that he owned part of her soul. Afterwards Carina had been so distraught no one had accused her of not looking after her little cousin properly. Carina, after all, had been only nine. But she could swim and swim well. She'd said fright had frozen her in place, making her incapable of jumping into the water after her cousin.

It had taken Bryn to do that.

'Thank God for you, Bryn! I'll never forget this. Never!' A weeping Elizabeth Forsyth had looked deep into his eyes, cradling Francey's small body in her arms as though Francey was the only child she had.

Carina had been standing nearby. He had already calmed Francey, who had clung to him like a little monkey, coughing up water, trying so hard to be brave. That was when the main party had arrived, alerted by his long, carrying *co-ee,* the traditional cry for help in the bush. All of them had huddled prayerfully around them. Catastrophe had been averted.

'How did you know they were here, Bryn?' Elizabeth had asked in wonder. 'We all thought they'd gone back to the main camp.' That was where a large tent had been erected.

'The old woman spoke and I listened.' It had been an odd thing to say, but no one had laughed.

Aborigines had an uncanny sense of danger. More so of approaching death. The old woman had even sent a strong wind at his back, though such a wind blew in no other place in the area. When everyone returned to the campsite to thank the old woman she'd been nowhere to be found. Even afterwards the aboriginal people who crisscrossed the station on walkabout claimed to know nothing of her or her whereabouts.

The wind blew her in. The wind blew her out.

'Coulda been a ghost!' Eddie Emu, one of the stockmen, had told them without a smile. 'Ghosts take all forms, ya know!'

Magic and the everyday were interconnected with aboriginal people. One had to understand that. Eddie claimed to have seen the spirit of his dead wife many times in an owl. That was why the owl took its rest by day and never slept at night. Owls hovered while men slept. Owls gave off signals, messages.

All in all it had been an extraordinary day. Little trembling Francey had whispered something into his ear that day. Something that had always remained with him.

'Carrie walked into the water. I did too.'

So what in God's name had really happened? Simply a child's terrible mistake? His mind had shut down on any other explanation. Carina had not been sufficiently aware of the danger and had later told fibs to exonerate herself from blame. It was a natural enough instinct.

Bryn came on them exactly where Jili had told him: Wungulla Lagoon, where the great corroborees had once been held. He seriously doubted whether a corroboree would be held to mark Sir Frank's passing. Francis Forsyth had not been loved, nor respected in the purest sense. Feared, most certainly. It hadn't taken the station people half a minute to become aware of Sir Frank's dark streak. Everyone had obeyed him. No one had trusted him. Who could blame them? He himself had not trusted Francis Forsyth for many years now.

He parked the Jeep a short distance off, approaching on foot and dodging the great mushrooming mounds of spinifex, bright green instead of the usual burnt gold. Francey was in the middle of a group of women, five in all, all busy at their painting. They looked totally involved, perfectly in harmony with their desert home.

Francey might have nearly drowned in Koopali Lagoon at age six, but at twenty-three she was a bush warrior. She could swim like a fish. She was fearless in an uncompromising environment that could and did take lives. She could handle the swiftest and strongest horse on the station. She could ride bareback if she had to, and find her way in the wilderness. She could shoot and hunt if it became necessary. In fact she was a crack shot, with an excellent eye. She knew all about bush tucker—how to make good bread from very finely ground small grass seeds, where to find the wild limes and figs, the bush tomatoes and a whole supermarket of wild berries and native fruits. Francey knew how to survive. She had made friends with the aboriginal people from her earliest childhood. In turn they had taught her a great deal about their own culture, without compromising the secrets forbidden to white people. They had taught her to see *their* landscape with her own eyes. And now she had a highly recognisable painting style that was bringing in excellent reviews.

Over the past few years since she had left university as one of the top three graduates in law for her year—Francey had thought it necessary to know her way around big business and the administration of her own sizeable trust fund—she had begun to capture the fantasy of aboriginal mythology with her own acutely imaginative vision. Her paintings—Bryn loved them, and owned quite a few—were a deeply sensitive and sympathetic mix of both cultures. She'd already had one sellout showing, stressing to press and collectors alike the great debt she owed to her aboriginal mentors. As it happened all of them were women, who were now commanding quite a following thanks to their own talent and Francesca's endeavours. Aboriginal art *was* extraordinarily powerful.

She rose to her feet the moment the Jeep came into view. She was walking towards him, as graceful as a gazelle. She had the Forsyth height— tall for a woman—and willow-slender beautiful limbs. Her face was protected by an attractive wide- brimmed hat made of woven grasses, probably fashioned for her by one of the women. Her long shiny river of hair, that when loose fell into deep lustrous waves, was caught back into a thick rope that trailed down her back. A single silky skein lay across her throat like a ribbon. She wore the simplest of gear: a pale blue cotton shirt streaked with paint, beige shorts, dusty trainers on her feet.

'Bryn!' she called.

Her voice, one of her great attractions, was like some lovely musical instrument.

'Hi there, Francey!'

Just the sight of her set up a curious ache deep inside him. He knew what it meant. Of course he did. But how did he turn things around? They stood facing each other. Their eyes met. Instant communication. And they both *knew* it—however hard she tried to disguise it. She lifted her face to him and kissed his cheek.

The cool satin touch of her flesh! He could see the flush of blood beneath her smooth golden skin before the familiar dissembling began. Both of them seemed to be stuck in roles imposed on them from childhood. That would change now.

'It has to be something serious to bring you here, Bryn.' She held her tapering long-fingered hands in front of her in an instinctive gesture of defensiveness. 'It's Grandfather, isn't it?' She turned her head abruptly, as if responding to a signal. The women were still sitting in their painting circle, but they had all left off work. Now they lifted their hands high in unison, palms facing upwards to the sky.

Now we have moved to an end.

Bryn recognised and wasn't greatly surprised by the ceremonial gesture. These people were extraordinary. 'Yes, Francey, it is,' he confirmed gravely. 'Your grandfather died of a massive heart attack yesterday afternoon. I came as quickly as I could. I'm very sorry for your pain. I know you can only be thinking of what might have been.'

'I wasn't *there,* Bryn.' Her voice splintered in her throat. 'I knew the moment I saw you what you were going to tell me.'

'I'm sorry, Francey,' he repeated. 'You're getting so close to these people you're acquiring their powers. How do *they* know? It's not guesswork. They *know.*'

'Uncanny, isn't it?' She flung another glance over her shoulder. The women had resumed their painting. 'But then they're the oldest living culture on earth. They've lived right *here* on this spot for over forty thousand years. They can scent death.'

He nodded. He had seen it happen many times. His eyes remained locked on her. She had lost colour at his news, but she was pushing away the tears. She wore no make-up that he could see, beyond lipgloss to protect her mouth. Her skin was flawless, poreless—like a baby's. Her large almond-shaped eyes, heavily and blackly lashed, dazzled like silver coins in the sunlight.

'He didn't want to see me?' It came out on a wave of sadness and deep regret.

Bryn found himself, as ever, protective. He hastened to explain. 'It wasn't a case of his wanting to see anyone, Francey.' He knew the hurt and pain of exclusion she had carried for most of her life. 'It happened at a board meeting, not at the house. None of us had the slightest idea he was feeling unwell. One moment he was shouting Charles down—a bit of an argument had started up, nothing really, but you know how he detests…detested…any other view but his own—and that was it. It was very quick. I doubt he felt more than a moment's pain. We didn't contact you right away because I wanted to tell you in person. I have to bring you home. He's being given a State funeral.'

'I suppose he would be!' A deep sigh escaped her. 'What great wealth and politics can do! As for home…' Sudden tears made her eyes shimmer like foil. 'That word should mean *everything*. It's meaningless to me. I don't have a home. I never had a home since I lost my parents.' She cast him a despairing look. 'I spent my childhood trying to find a way through grief. I had to focus on what my father once said to me when I was little and a wasp stung me. "Be brave, Francey, darling. Be brave."'

'You *are* brave, Francey,' Bryn said, knowing that for all the Forsyth wealth she had had a difficult life.

Her beautiful eyes glistened with blinked-back tears. 'Well, I try. Some of the worst things happen to us in childhood. Sadly I haven't left mine entirely behind. Carina used to tell me all the time I should be grateful.'

'Well, that's Carina!' he said, unable to keep the harsh edge from his voice.

Francesca was vaguely shocked. Bryn *never* criticised Carina. Not to date. 'I don't think she was trying to upset me, Bryn,' she pointed out loyally. 'She meant me to buck up. But enough of that.' She made a dismissive gesture with her hand. 'I don't often feel sorry for myself. But Grandfather's death has come as a shock. He lived like he truly believed he was going to go on for ever. Well into his nineties at any rate. I'm very grateful you've come, Bryn.'

He shook his uncovered dark head, sunlight striking bronze highlights. 'No need for gratitude, Francey. I wanted to come.'

She gave a broken laugh that ended on a sob. 'You and your family grew much closer to me than my own. Isn't that incredible? I'm so grateful you were there for me.'

He heard the affection and sincerity in her voice. His mother and grandmother always had been strongly but subtly protective of Francesca, careful not to show their resentments of the Forsyths. Now an opportunity had opened up and he had to take it.

'We've never spoken about this, Francey, and you probably don't want to hear it from me now, but Carina isn't quite the friend you think she is.'

She didn't look at all shocked by his comment. She looked ineffably sad.

'Why *is* that, Bryn?' she asked in a pained voice.

'I've never done anything—never would do anything—to hurt Carina. I've been extremely careful to stay in the background. I don't compete in any way. *She* is the Forsyth heiress, not me. And I don't want to be. I try to live my own life. Whenever we have to attend functions together I never draw attention to myself. I always dress down.'

'You should stop that,' he said, more bluntly than he'd intended.

Now she did look shocked. 'You think so?' She sounded hurt.

'I do,' he told her more gently. 'No one could fail to see how beautiful you are, Francey, even in that bush shirt and shorts. You shouldn't be driven into playing down your looks or your own unique style.'

She blushed at the *beautiful*. Better maybe that he hadn't said it.

'It seemed to make good sense to me,' she confessed, rather bleakly.

'Yes, I know.' He studied her downbent face. 'You had your reasons. But I don't believe it would make a difference anyway.' He decided to turn up the heat one more degree. Jili's warnings were still resounding in his ears. 'Carina believes you stole her mother's love from her. That's at the heart of it all.'

Her luminous gaze swept his face. 'But that's a terrible burden to lay on me. I was a child. Five years of age. I was a victim. I never wanted my parents to die. It was the great tragedy of my life. Losing my grandfather here and now, painful and sudden as it is, in no way compares. The worst thing that can happen to you only happens *once*. I'm sorry for the way that sounds, but I can't be hypocritical about it. Grandfather never loved me. He never wanted *my* love. He never showed me any real affection. The only time I got treated as a granddaughter was when we were all on show. Just a piece of play-acting, a side-show. I was his granddaughter by chance. I'm not blonde and blue-eyed like the Forsyths. I'm my mother's child. And I lost her. *Still* Carina can resent me?'

Hate you, more like it. 'I'm afraid so. Carina's resentments are not of your making, Francey, so don't look so upset. It's her nature. She's inherited the Forsyth dark side.'

'But surely that must be a cause of grief to her?' she said, her voice full of pity for her cousin.

'I don't think she sees it like that,' he responded tersely, alarmed that Francesca's innate sense of compassion should work against her. 'One has to have an insight into one's own behaviour. I don't think Carina has that. I'm glad this is out in the open, Francey, because we both know there will be tough times ahead. It's best to prepare for them.'

'She must be terribly upset.' She fixed her eyes on him. 'Carrie idolised Grandfather.'

'She's coping,' he said.

'That's good. Carrie is very strong. And she has you. She loves *you*,' Francesca added softly, as though offering the best possible reason for Carina to be strong.

Why did people think Carina Forsyth was the fixed star in Bryn's firmament? Francesca thought it the most. 'She only *thinks* she loves me, Francey.' His retort was crisp. He didn't say love wasn't in Carina's heart or soul. Carina wanted what she couldn't have. It was a psychological problem.

'It's not as simple as that, Bryn,' Francesca contradicted him gently. 'You're very close. She told me you were lovers.' Her voice was low, but her light-sparked eyes were steady.

'Okay.' He shrugged, his voice perfectly calm. 'So we were. Things happen. But that was a few years back.'

'She says *not*.' It wasn't like Bryn to lie.

Francesca had long since made the judgment that Bryn had no time for lies.

He couldn't suppress the sudden flare of anger. It showed in his brilliant dark eyes. 'And of course you believe her?'

Her lovely face flamed. 'You're saying it's *not* the truth?' Momentarily she came out from behind her habitual screen.

For answer he flashed a smile that lit up his stunning, lean-featured face. It was a face that could in repose look somewhat severe—even at times as hard and formidable as Francis Forsyth himself. 'Francey, I'm a free man. I like it that way.'

'You might not always feel the same, and Carina will be waiting for you.' She pulled her sunglasses out of her pocket and hid behind the dark lenses. 'Do you want to say hello to the group?'

'Of course. I wouldn't think of bypassing them.'

He moved alongside her as they made their way back to the artists at work. Their only protection from the brassy glare of the sun was a magnificent overhanging desert oak. In cities nature was controlled. In the Outback it manifested its tremendous intensity and power.

'I see Nellie is here today,' he commented. Nellie Napirri, a tribal woman of indeterminate age—anywhere between seventy and ninety— generally focused on the flora and fauna of the riverine desert. The great Monet himself might have been interested in seeing her huge canvases of waterlilies, Bryn thought. As well as using traditional earth pigments, the familiar ochres, she used vibrant acrylics to express her Dreaming.

'I thought we might have seen the last of her,' Francesca confided. 'Nellie is a real nomad. But she came back. She'd been on a very long walkabout that took her up into the Territory. Imagine walking all that way. And at her age! Goodness knows how old she is. She's been around for as long as anyone can remember. It's unbelievable.'

Bryn's mind was swept back to the day when Francesca had almost drowned, but for miraculous intervention. He vividly remembered the old woman—the way she had vanished from the face of the earth but had in all probability gone walkabout. For him that day had amounted to a religious experience. He could still see Carina's small straight back, her long blonde hair cascading over her shoulders. She had been facing Koopali, fixed to the ground. He would never forget the way she had started screaming…

The little group of painters, gracious and well-mannered, came to their feet, exchanging hand-shakes with Bryn. Four pairs of eyes fixed themselves on him.

'Big fella bin gone,' Nellie announced in a deep quiet voice. Her curly head was snow-white, her eyes remarkably clear and sharp for so old a woman. It was obvious she had been appointed spokeswoman.

Bryn inclined his dark head in salute. 'Yesterday, Nellie. A massive heart attack. I'm here to take Francesca back with me.'

Nellie reached out and touched his arm. 'Better here,' she said, frowning darkly, as though seriously concerned for Francesca's welfare. She searched Bryn's face so carefully she might have been seeing him for the first time. Or was she trying to see into his soul? 'Your job look after her, *byamee*.'

'Don't worry, Nellie, I will,' he answered gravely. He knew *byamee* was a term of respect—a name given to someone of high degree. He only hoped he would be worthy of that honour. He recalled with a sharp pang of grief that the tribal people had called his grandfather *byamee*. He had never in all the long years heard it applied to Sir Frank.

A look of relief settled on Nellie's wise old face.

'You remember now. I bin telling ya. *Not over.*' All of a sudden her breath began to labour.

Francesca reacted at once. 'Nellie, dear, you mustn't worry. Everything is going to be fine.' She drew the tiny bent frame beneath her arm. 'Now, why don't we show Bryn what we've been doing?' she suggested bracingly. 'You know how much he loves and appreciates indigenous art.'

It sprang to Bryn's mind how Carina had once passed off her young cousin's desire to promote the work of indigenous artists as 'trying to exorcise the fact she's an heiress by working among the aborigines.'

Carina wasn't only callous, she could be remarkably blind—especially when it came to perceiving what was *good*. She was no judge of Francesca's work. Francesca Forsyth was a multi-gifted young woman. His mind ran back to the many times he and Francey had got into discussions, not only about Titan, but about the various projects handled—or mishandled might be a better word—by the Forsyth Foundation. Francey had a seriously good brain. When he was in a position to do so, he would endeavour to get her elected to the board, no matter her youth. Hell, he was still considered very young himself, though youth wasn't the issue it once was. It was more about ability. And Francey was ready for it. She had inherited her father Lionel's formidable head for business. His grandmother had confirmed that with an ironic smile.

'When it comes right down to it Francey, not Carina, would make the greatest contribution. Only as fate would have it Carina is the apple of Frank's eye. He never was much of a judge of character.'

It was as they were taking their leave that Nellie found a moment to speak to Bryn alone. She raised her snowy white head a long way, trying to look him squarely in the eye. 'You bin her family now,' she said, as though impressing on him his responsibility. 'Others gunna do all in their power to destroy her.'

'Nellie—'

She cut him off. 'You know that well as me. She sees good in everyone. Even those who will turn against her.'

He already knew that. 'They will seek to destroy me too, Nellie.' He spoke as if she were not a nomadic tribal woman but a trusted business ally. Moreover he saw nothing incongruous about it.

These people had many gifts. Prescience was a part of them.

'Won't happen,' she told him, her weathered face creasing with scorn. 'You strong. You bin ready. This time you get justice.'

She might have been delivering a speech, and it was one he heard loud and clear.

They were in the station Jeep, speeding back to the homestead, with the silver-shot mirage pulsing all around them. The native drums had started up, reverberating across the plains to the ancient eroded hills glowing fiery red in the heat. Other drums were joining in, taking up the beat— *tharum, tharum*—a deeply primitive sound that was extraordinarily thrilling. They were calling back and forth to each other, seemingly from miles away. The sound came from the North, the North-West.

It was a signal, Bryn and Francesca realised. Now that Bryn's coming had made it official, the message was being sent out over the vast station and the untameable land.

Francis Forsyth's spirit had passed. Consequences would follow.

'Nellie fears for me,' Francesca said. 'It looked

like she was handing on lots of warnings to you?'
Her tone pressed him for information.

'Your well-being is important to her and her
friends.' Bryn glanced back at her. She had taken
off her straw hat, throwing it onto the back seat.
Now he could fully appreciate her beautiful fine-
boned face, which always seemed to him radiant
with sensitivity. She was far more beautiful than
her cousin. Her looks were on a different scale.
The thick shiny rope of her hair was held by a
coloured elastic band at the end and a blue and
purple silk scarf at the top. Incredibly, her eyes had
taken on a wash of violet. 'You've been wonderfully helpful to them as a patron, and best of all
your motives are entirely pure.'

'Of course they are.' She dismissed that important point as if it went without saying. 'It looked
like matters of grave importance?'

'Isn't your welfare just that?' he parried.

'Who is likely to hurt me?' she appealed to him.
'I'm not important in anyone's eyes—least of all
poor Grandfather. God rest his troubled soul. I do
know he had his bad times.'

Why wouldn't he? Bryn inwardly raged, but let
it go. 'You're a Forsyth, Francey,' he reminded her
gravely. 'It's to be expected you'll receive a sub-

stantial fortune in your grandfather's will. It's not as though there isn't plenty to go around. He was a billionaire many times over.'

'A huge responsibility!' There was a weight of feeling in her voice. 'Too much money is a curse. Men who build up great fortunes make it extremely difficult for their heirs.'

She was thinking of her uncle Charles. So was Bryn. 'I think there's an old proverb, either Chinese or Persian, that says: "The larger a man's roof, the more snow it collects." Charles, God help him, has had a bad time of it. I can almost feel sorry for him. Frank treated him very unkindly from his earliest days. Charles never could measure up to his father's standards of perfection.'

'Such destructive behaviour,' Francesca sighed, thinking that at least her uncle treated Carina, his only child, like a princess.

'I agree. It was *your* father who inherited the brains and refused point-blank to toe the line. It took a lot of guts to do that. Charles has worked very hard, but sadly for him he doesn't have what it takes to be the man at the top. Charles is just valued for his *name.*'

Unfortunately that was true. 'Our name engenders a lot of hostility.' She had felt that hostility herself. 'It's not *all* envy. The Macallan name, on the other hand, is greatly admired. Sir Theo was revered.'

'A great philanthropist,' Bryn said quietly, immensely proud of his grandfather.

'And a great *man*. He had no black cloud hanging over him. I've never fully understood what my grandfather did to your family after Sir Theo died. No one speaks of it.'

'And I'm not going to speak of it now, Francey,' he said, severity back on him. 'It's a bad day for it anyway.'

'I know. I know,' she apologised. 'But you haven't put it behind you?'

'Far from it.' He suddenly turned his smooth dark head, so elegantly shaped. '*You* could be the enemy.'

She looked out of the window at the desert landscape that had come so wondrously alive. 'You know I'm not.' She loved him without limit. Always would.

He laughed briefly. 'You're certainly not typical of the Forsyths.' She was the improbable angel in their midst.

Her next words were hard for her to say. 'You hate us?' It was very possible. She knew Lady

Macallan had despised her grandfather with a passion. There had to be a story there.

A shadow moved across his handsome face. 'I can't hate *you,* Francey. How could you even think it?'

She sighed. 'Besides, how could you hate me when you own half my soul?' She spoke with intensity. But then, wasn't that the way it always felt when she was with Bryn? The heightened perceptions, every nerve ending wired?

'Do you believe it?' He turned his dark head again to meet her eyes.

'I wouldn't be here without *you,* Bryn,' she said, on a soft expelled breath. 'I like to think we're…friends.'

'Well, we are,' he replied, somewhat sardonically. 'I want you to promise me something, Francey.'

Something in his tone alarmed her. 'If I can,' she answered warily.

'You *must,*' he clipped out, abruptly steering away from a red-glowing boulder that crouched like some mythical animal in the jungle of green gilt-tipped grasses. 'If you're worried or unsure about something, or if you need someone to talk to, I want you to contact me. Will you do that?' There was a note of urgency in his voice.

'I promise.'

He shot her a brilliant glance that affected her powerfully. 'You mean that?'

'Absolutely. I never break a promise. A promise is like a vow.'

'So let's shake on it.' He hit the brake and brought the vehicle to a stop in the shade of a stand of bauhinias, the branches lavishly decorated with flowers of purest white and lime-green. 'Give me your hand.'

On the instant her heart began fluttering wildly, as if a small bird was trapped in her chest. She was crazily off guard. She only hoped her face wasn't betraying the turmoil within her. 'Okay,' she managed at last. She gave him her hand. Skin on skin. She had to fight hard to compose herself. Beneath her reserved façade she went in trepidation of Bryn Macallan and his power over her. So much so she feared to be alone with him, even though she spent countless hours wishing she were.

But how did one stop longing for what one so desperately longed for?

Bryn's hand was gripping hers—not gently, but tightly. It was as though he wanted her to understand what her promise might mean in the days ahead.

To Francesca the intimacy was breathtaking.

The heat in her blood wrapped her body like a shawl. Her limbs were melting, as though her body might collapse like a concertina. For glittering moments she accepted her deepest longings and desires. She was irrevocably in love with Bryn Macallan. She couldn't remember a time she hadn't been. It was the most important thing in her life. She was off her head, really. And it was *so* humiliating. Carina was the woman in Bryn's life. She had to clamp down on the torment.

'Where will it finally end, Francey?' Bryn was asking quietly, not relinquishing her hand as she'd thought he would. 'You know I mean to take over Titan?'

He waited in silence for her response. 'I'm aware of your burning ambitions, Bryn,' she said. 'I know you want to put things *right*. I don't know your secrets, and you won't tell me, but I do know you would probably have the numbers to oust Uncle Charles.'

'Without a doubt!' Not the slightest flare of arrogance, just plain fact, though the muscles along his jaw clenched.

'Grandfather's dearest wish was for you and Carina to marry.' She turned to look him squarely in the face. 'To unite the two dynasties.'

'I'm well aware of that,' he answered, his tone suggesting her grandfather's dearest wish didn't come into it.

Or so she interpreted it. Was she wrong? 'And it will happen?'

If for whatever reason the longed-for alliance didn't eventuate, he knew Carina would become his enemy. He laughed, but there was little humour in it. 'Why don't you leave all that to me, Francey? My main concern at the moment is *you.*'

Heat started up in her veins. 'Me?' She was unable to find another word.

'Yes, you. Don't sound so surprised. I don't see much of you. Certainly not as much as I'd like,' Bryn continued as she remained silent. He firmed up his hold on her trembling hand, then—shockingly—raised it to his lips.

'*"Thus with a kiss I die."*' he quoted lightly, but Francesca's heart flipped in her breast.

It was easy to identify Romeo's final line. What was Bryn thinking, saying that? It bewildered her. So did his darkly enigmatic gaze. Didn't he know how difficult it was for her, loving him and knowing he was with Carina? But then, how *could* he know? She did everything possible to hide her true feelings.

'Break out of your shell, Francesca,' he abruptly urged. 'You've been over-long inside it.'

She felt a rush of humiliation at the criticism. Doubly so because he was right. 'I thought it was for my own protection.'

'I understand all that.'

There was a high, humming sound in her ears. 'May I have my hand back?'

'Of course.' He released her hand on the instant, leaning forward to switch on the ignition. 'We should get back anyway,' he added briskly. 'I want to leave as soon as possible.'

'I'm ready.'

It wasn't a good feeling.

She could feel her heart sink.

The Jeep bounded across the vast sun-drenched plain accompanied by a great flight of budgerigars—the phenomenon of the Outback that had materialised again. Francesca gazed up at them, wondering if and when she would see Daramba again. She was certain her uncle would inherit the pastoral chain, but Charles had never much cared for Daramba.

Like all inhabitants of the great island continent, in particular of remote Western Australia, he was used to vast open spaces, to incredible *emptiness,* but on his own admission something about Daramba spooked him. It was there, after all, that Gulla Nolan had mysteriously disappeared. The verdict after an intensive search at the time was that Gulla had been drunk and had slipped into one of the maze of waterholes, billabongs, lagoons and swamps that criss-crossed the station. Everyone knew Gulla had had a great liking for the booze. Gulla Nolan had been the famous tracker Sir Theodore Macallan and her own grandfather had taken along with them on their expeditions. Gulla had been with them when they had discovered Mount Gloriana.

To this day no one knew Gulla's fate—although it was Sir Theo who had set up a trust fund which had grown very substantially over the years, for Gulla and his descendants. One of them was a well-known political activist—a university graduate, educated through the Gulla Nolan Trust and—ironically—a sworn enemy of the Forsyths. It was quite possible, then, that her uncle would sell Daramba, if not the whole chain.

CHAPTER TWO

THE funeral of Sir Francis Forsyth was unique in one respect. No one cried. Though it should be said there was no easy way to shed a tear for a man more often described as 'a ruthless bastard' than a jewel in the giant State of Western Australia's crown. Nevertheless, the Anglican Cathedral St George's—Victorian Gothic Revival in style, and relatively modest compared to the huge Catholic Cathedral, St Mary's, built on the site that had actually been set aside by the Founding Fathers for St George's—was packed by 'mourners'. This covered anyone who was anyone in the public eye: a federal senator, representative of the Prime Minister, the State Premier, the State Governor, who had once privately called Sir Francis 'an appalling old villain', various dignitaries, representatives of the pastoral, business and the legal world. All seated behind the Forsyth family on the right, the Macallan family to the left.

The truly ironic thing was that Sir Theodore Macallan, co-founder with Sir Francis of Titan, had been universally loved and admired. But then, Sir Theo had been a great man, with that much-to-be-desired accolade of being a true *gentleman* bestowed on him. That meant a gentleman at *heart* as well as in the graciousness of his manner. It had helped that he had been a huge benefactor to the state as well. Sir Frank, on the other hand, had always kept his philanthropy in line with tax avoidance schemes—all legal, naturally. He had long been known to proclaim he paid his taxes along with everyone else, of course. One didn't get to be a billionaire and not have an army of lawyers whose whole lives were devoted to protecting the Forsyth business empire against all comers—including the government.

The Forsyth heiress, Carina, looked *wonderful,* they all agreed. Everyone craned their heads for a look, even though footage of the celebrity funeral would appear on national television.

The whole funeral scene had been revolutionised over recent years: the style of eulogies, the music that would never have been allowed in the old days, the kind of people given the opportunity to speak, even the things they got away with saying. The entire ritual had been rewritten. And today most of the mourners, some of whom had expressed behind-the-scenes opinions that the world was a better place without the deceased, had dressed up as much as they would have if they'd been going to a huge social function like the Melbourne Cup. There was even the odd whiff of excitement in the air. Many, on meeting up with old friends, had to concentrate hard on not breaking into laughter, though some light laughter would be allowed during the eulogies.

Carina Forsyth attracted the most attention. She always wore the most glamorous clothes and jewels—even to her grandfather's funeral. Everyone looked at the size of her South Sea pearls, a steal at $100,000 a strand! The state had always been famous for its pearling industry. No one was about to bring up a fairly recent scandal when a society wife—present on this sad day— had accused the heiress of having an affair with her businessman husband and labelled her 'a tramp.' Well, not today anyway. Not before, during or after the service. Possibly over drinks that evening.

The 'spare' Forsyth heiress, as Francesca had long been dubbed by the press, by comparison was very plainly attired. A simple black suit, modest jewellery, no big glamorous hat, and her long hair arranged in a low coil at her nape, held with a stylised black grosgrain ribbon. She even wore sunglasses in church—a sure sign she wanted to hide. Not that the 'spare' needed to hide. Francesca Forsyth had already established herself in the general community's good books. As a Forsyth, like her cousin, it wouldn't have been necessary for her ever to lift a finger, but Francesca was creating a real niche for herself in public-spirited good works—like the aunt who had reared her, the much admired Elizabeth Forsyth, who—oddly—was seated with the Macallans. Then again, everyone knew about the split in the Forsyth family ranks.

While Carina was feted, and treated with a near sickening degree of deference—at least to her face—her cousin was winning for herself a considerable degree of affection and admiration of which she was unaware.

What everyone needed to know now was this: what were the contents of Sir Francis Forsyth's will? It was taken for granted that his only son Charles Forsyth would be the main beneficiary, though Charles had always been judged by the business community as 'dead wood'. There were all sorts of interlocking trusts in place to provide income for various members of the extended family, but the bulk of the Forsyth fortune would pass by tradition to his eldest son—Sir Francis's younger son, Lionel, with whom he had fallen out anyway, being deceased.

The entire business world could clearly see Charles Forsyth's clear and present danger. He was sitting in the front pew on the left.

Tall, stunningly handsome, powerfully lean and sombre of expression, Bryn sat between his aristocratic grandmother, Lady Antonia Macallan, and his beautiful mother, Annette Macallan, who had never remarried despite the many offers that had followed in the wake of the tragic death of her husband. Bryn Macallan was firmly entrenched as a power player. It was said he had handled without effort everything the late Sir Francis had thrown at him—and Sir Francis had done a lot of throwing. Considered one of the biggest catches in the country, he was not yet married. Everyone in the state knew Sir Francis had worked for an alliance—a business merger—between Macallan and his granddaughter Carina, but so far nothing had eventuated. It was generally held that it was only a question of *when*.

The mining giant Titan was too big to be owned by any one family—indeed, any one person—but Macallan, through his family history, his prodigious intellect and business acumen, looked very much as if he could at some stage become the man in control. Surely that was reason enough for him and Carina Forsyth to finally tie the knot? Both of them had 'star quality'.

Hundreds of people flocked back to the Forsyth mansion, a geometric modern-day fortress, wandering all over the huge reception rooms and the library as if it was open house and the property would soon be up for auction. Very few of them had ever been invited inside, so most faces were stamped with expressions of wonderment, amazement and occasionally dismay—but huge curiosity none the less.

Although the day was quite hot, Charles Forsyth stood in front of a gigantic stone fireplace—one might wonder from whence it had been acquired…from one of the Medici clan, probably—looking chilled to the bone. The aperture, filled on that day with a stupendous arrangement of white lilies and fanning greenery, was so vast a fully grown man could have been roasted standing up.

'Buck up, Dad, for God's sake!' Carina uttered a wrathful warning into her father's ear. Though she loved her father, sometimes his manner simply enraged her. She quite understood how it had enraged her grandfather.

'The devil with that!' her father replied. 'I've seen the will.'

'So?' Carina drew back, as if a particularly virulent wasp, hidden away in the lilies, had chosen that moment to sting her. 'It's what we expected, isn't it?'

'No, it isn't,' Charles Forsyth admitted, his face abruptly turning red.

Carina turned her back to the huge crowded living room, squarely facing her father. Her eyes had turned a chilling iceberg blue. 'So *when* were you going to tell *me?*'

Her tone was so trenchant, so much like his father's, that for a moment Charles Forsyth looked terrified. 'You'll know soon enough. I wish you weren't so much like him, Carrie. It frightens me sometimes. You're right. I should buck up and circulate. Most of them have only come to goggle and giggle anyway. This place *is* in appalling taste. Forget any notion Dad was revered, or even liked. Even the Archbishop was hard-pressed to come up with the odd kind word. My father has the rankest outside chance of getting into heaven.'

Carina gritted her perfect white teeth. 'Get a grip, Dad! There *is* no heaven.'

He laughed sadly. 'You may be right. But there is, God help us, a hell. There's no glory in *inheriting* a great fortune, Carina. Whatever you believe. You've no idea of normal life because you've been so pampered. Nothing has been expected of you except to look glamorous. The job of stepping into your grandfather's shoes is bigger than you and I can possibly imagine. I'll be the first to admit I don't have the intellect. And I'm far from tough. Everyone knows my bark is worse than my bite. We need someone as tough as he was, even when he *was* slowing down. He knew it himself. He was coming to rely more and more on Macallan's judgment, and the good will that goes with the Macallan name. Sir Theo *wasn't* a scoundrel.'

It took all of Carina's self-control not to lash out in anger. She had adored her grandfather. She *adored* strength and ruthlessness in a man. They were assets, not mortal sins. 'I'm not going to listen to this!' she said, her eyes turning hard and cold as stones. 'Gramps was a great man.'

'That's your view, certainly,' her father answered wearily. 'But you won't find many to agree with you.' For a minute Charles Forsyth was almost tempted to tell his daughter just a few of her grandfather's venial sins, even if he left out the mortal ones. But what purpose would that serve? 'We owe our great success in the main to Sir Theo,' he told his daughter patiently. 'We owe him many times over. What we need now is a *fighter!* You must be aware Orion is awaiting its opportunity to move in on us? I'm not a fighter. I'm a coward. Your mother told me that at the end, before the divorce. I have no guts. She was right. She was always right.'

'Leave Mum out of this,' Carina said furiously. 'She betrayed us both when she left you. See the way she was sitting with the Macallans? Hiding behind that black veil? She hated Gramps.'

'And she despised *me* while she was at it,' Charles Forsyth said sadly. 'I don't blame her. Every time Dad bawled me out I crumpled like a soggy sponge. I spent a lifetime being despised by my father. I was so in awe of him, so desperate to please him, I never got a chance to develop my own character. Can I help it if with his passing it seems like an intolerable burden has been lifted from my shoulders—?' He broke off, as if exhausted. 'The best thing you can possibly do, Carrie, for yourself and for the rest of us is get Macallan to marry you. That would solve *all* our problems. He's a man who could handle the Forsyth Foundation as well. But Macallan doesn't seem to be in any rush to ask you.'

That touched an agonisingly raw nerve. 'Keep out of it, Dad,' Carina warned, staring at her father with something approaching ferocity. 'I'll handle this in my own way.'

'No doubt!' Charles shot a troubled glance across the room, to where Bryn Macallan was standing in quiet conversation with his niece, Francesca. Macallan's height and his superb athletic build made Francesca, who was tall for a woman, look as fragile as a lily on a stalk. Beautiful girl, Francesca. Totally different style from his daughter. Far more elegant, he suddenly realised. And so much more to her. Already at twenty-three she was making quite a name for herself as an artist. Not that any of that mattered any more...

Carina's gaze had followed her father's, because she always followed Bryn and Francey's whereabouts. 'Just like Gramps didn't tell you everything, neither do I. Sometimes it's best *not* to know. Francey's no threat, if that thought has ever crossed your mind. It's *me* Bryn wants, but he needs to bring me to heel. I rather like that.' She gave her father a vixen's smile. It was more chilling than her glare.

For some years now it had been Charles Forsyth's worst nightmare that his daughter would morph into his father. It was happening right in front of his eyes.

'There is a bond between them, you know.' Unwisely he found himself pointing it out. 'Bryn did save Francey's life all those years ago.'

Carina's eyes flashed blue lightning. 'Bryn—always the hero! Dear little Francey had taken Mum over even *then.*'

Charles Forsyth was shocked by her tone. 'Nothing deliberate, Carrie. Francesca was such a *lovely* child.'

'And *I* wasn't?' Carina asked fiercely, her creamy flushed cheeks only heightening her knock-out beauty.

'Of course you were. You were perfect. You *are* perfect,' her father lied desperately. Often as a child Carina had been truly horrible. Once she had even ransacked her mother's study. *Horrible!* 'Poor little Francey was an orphan,' he said, in an effort to win his niece some sympathy. 'She was in desperate need of tender loving care, which your mother gave her. You were *never* neglected, Carrie. Not for one moment. Why do you blame your cousin so? She was the innocent victim.'

'Actually, *I* was the victim,' Carina said, never more serious in her life. 'Though you and Mum never noticed. Francey was no innocent. She might have started out that way, but as time went on she and Mum were always in league in a conspiracy against me.'

Charles Forsyth was torn two ways. Between love for his daughter and a growing fear that he didn't really know or possibly even *like* her. 'That's not right, Carrie! You should speak to someone about this. What you have is a phobia, and it seems to be growing worse.'

Carina laughed. 'Sorry, Dad, but I'm spot-on. Mum lived for Francey. Think of it! My own mother loves my cousin far more than she loves me, her only child.'

'Maybe you wouldn't let her love you?' her father countered.

'How could I, when she was always turning to Francey?' Carina answered, as though the explanation was obvious. She put up a hand to pat her father's cheek. Oddly, it caused him to jump as if she had administered an electric shock. 'Look, Dad, I love Francey. I admire her essential *goodness*. We're not only first cousins, we're the closest of friends. She often comes to me for advice, and I'm delighted to give it. I can't help it if occasionally I have a little growl about Mum's affection for her. I'm no saint.'

No, you're not, God help us! Charles Forsyth felt a blindingly sharp pain in his right temple. Lord knew what might happen if Macallan suddenly switched his attentions from Carina to Francesca. With all he now knew, it *could* happen. There were all sorts of surprises in life. A huge one was about to hit them like a tidal wave. And there would be hell to pay if ever Carina's plans were thwarted. Carina had a formidable array of weapons—not the least of them his father's legendary ruthlessness. *He* wouldn't want to be in the shoes of any woman who tried to oust Carina in Macallan's affections.

Now more than ever early retirement seemed a welcome option for Charles Forsyth. He was ready to quit the stage. He hadn't really needed to be shoved.

The reading of the will was set for an hour after the last mourner had left. Francesca thought she might faint away from distress and fatigue by then.

'Are you okay?' Bryn found her sitting quietly in a corner, partially obscured by a tall and luxuriant indoor palm. He drew up a chair beside her.

'Sort of,' she said, enormously grateful for his company. 'Death is very sobering, isn't it? What I profoundly regret is the fact I wasn't able to make a real connection with Grandfather and now I never will. But Carina was his great favourite, after all.'

'She was so like him,' Bryn offered by way of explanation.

Francesca smiled faintly. 'Yes. I always understood it was *my* job to keep quiet and out of the way. Lord knows how I would have turned out if not for Elizabeth and the innumerable kindnesses shown to me by your family. In a way—' she looked about them at the daunting opulence of the room '—I still feel like I'm in enemy territory in this great terrible house.'

'It is a bit of a monstrosity,' Bryn quietly agreed. He'd thought that the first time he had walked into the mansion all those years ago.

'I used to hope and pray Carrie and I might become inseparable,' Francesca confided poignantly. 'The two Forsyth girls.'

'It never happened.' A simple statement of fact.

'No. Our relationship, nevertheless, is close and binding. But somehow, underneath it all, I felt un-settled and confused. I'm much happier now living my own life, standing on my own two feet, looking to the future.'

'The future is what matters, Francey,' he told her, continuing to watch her closely. She was very pale, and far more genuinely upset than Carina. 'You have to let everything else—the bad things—recede into the past. Something inside tells me you're fated to be a powerful force for good.'

His comment made her heart topple. 'Oh, Bryn!' She waved an agitated hand, as if dismiss-ing the very idea.

'No, I mean it,' he said. 'You have a light around you, Francey. You did from your childhood. That light drew me to you.'

She was starting to feel really dizzy. 'You mean the day I nearly drowned?' What was going on inside his head? His heart? She couldn't be mistaken. There was a lot of feeling somewhere there.

'Then, and now,' he said.

She gave an involuntary shiver as memories crowded in. 'I often revisit that day in my dreams. The sense of danger is still with me.'

'Danger?' His black brows drew together in a frown. 'You've never spoken of it before.'

'So much I haven't put into words.' She sighed, feeling the weight of her suspicions. Carina, her own flesh and blood, a threat to her? Nothing good could possibly come out of saying that to Bryn. She knew better than anyone the relationship between Carina and him was too close. Her subconscious might grapple with her clouded memories, but she had to keep them under lock and key. Who would believe her anyway? She had often heard Carina describe her as 'nerve-ridden', all the while managing to sound deeply concerned. One thing was certain: exposing Carina could only bring heartbreak.

And trouble.

There was always that nagging thought. Crossing people like Carina, who thought what *she* wanted should be the law of the land, could develop into a life-threatening matter.

'No point in keeping it locked up inside you.' Bryn's frown darkened his handsome face. 'Better to speak to someone you trust about these things. I've told you I'm always ready to listen.'

'And I appreciate that, Bryn.' She made no attempt to conceal it. 'Life can be a lot tougher when you're rich.' She gave a little laugh, but the sound was very tense. She didn't want to be around for the will reading. She wanted to be well away.

Bryn briefly touched her hand, giving her his beautiful magnetic smile. 'Isn't that the truth? Look, you sit here quietly. I have to have a word with Frank's elder sister and her husband. But I'll be back.'

'Don't worry about me,' she said, realising her head was lolling slightly forward. 'I'll be fine.'

'I'll be back,' he repeated, looking every inch the hero.

Hang in there, Francey, she urged herself as Bryn walked away to join the Forsyths. *Everything passes.*

A moment later, Carina zoomed across the room to chide her. 'Don't droop, Francey. We have a duty to support one another.' Her eyes flicked over Francesca's slender figure. 'And couldn't you have done better than that suit? It's okay, I guess, but you try much too hard to pretend you don't have money when the whole damned country knows you have.'

'Perhaps you're right. Anyway, *you* look a billion dollars.'

'That's my job. Gramps took such pleasure in how

I looked. It's no easy task to look this good every day—especially when one has to attend the funeral of the person who loved me most in this world.'

Francesca realised that just might be true. 'I'm sorry, Carrie,' she murmured. 'Truly sorry. Grandfather did love you. He adored you.'

'And he would have loved you too, only there was always something *difficult* about you, Francey. You didn't fit in, and you never gave Gramps the reverence he deserved. He was a great man, yet that seemed to mean nothing to you.'

It took an effort, but Francesca had to deny the charge. 'That's not true. I gave Grandfather all the respect in the world. I couldn't rise to reverence. I associate reverence with saintly people—fallen war heroes, great humanitarians and the like. And, let's face it, I didn't have your wonderful self-assurance and I didn't have the Forsyth blonde, blue-eyed good-looks.'

'No, you missed out there. But you're attractive enough,' Carina told her, quite objectively. 'The pity of it is you don't do much for yourself.'

'Well, I intend to make a start,' Francesca said, making a visible effort to straighten her shoulders. 'Maybe tomorrow. I apologise if I'm looking a bit fraught. I haven't had much sleep.'

'And I have?' Carina cast her large blue eyes towards the ceiling. 'You do have dark circles under your eyes. No wonder you were hiding behind those sunglasses. Perhaps I should give you a good shake?' She glanced at Francesca sidelong. 'Remember how I used to shake you awake when we were kids? You used to keep me awake with your night terrors. Mum had fixed you up with a nightlight too. Sconces were left burning along the corridor, and if that weren't enough, I was in the next room. No one seemed to care much if *I* didn't like all that light shining in on me.'

'Poor, poor Carina. I do remember.' Francesca reached out a hand for the high back of a chair that really should have been in a museum to steady herself.

'You were always having such terrible dreams. What were they about? Nightmares about drowning?'

Why did Carina always bring that subject up? Was she constantly checking to see if Francesca's memory of the near tragedy remained dim?

'They were the worst.' Francesca gave a shudder. *Pitching or being pushed headlong into the dark green lagoon.* Even when she woke up she had felt bruised.

'Needless to say Mum always had to get up to comfort you. You weren't happy with little me. Mum had to come to pet you and soothe you back to sleep. Pathetic, really. Sometimes I used to think Mum loved you more than me.' She smiled into Francesca's eyes as if asking a question: what sort of mother would do that?

'Have a heart.' Francesca shook her aching head. 'I was only a little lost kid, Carrie. Your mother was just looking out for me.'

'Something she's doing to this day.' Carina only just succeeded in covering her intense resentment. 'Dad and I were terribly upset she sat with the Macallans. We could see that as a betrayal.'

'Perhaps Elizabeth wasn't prepared to be hypocritical?' Francesca suggested, loyal to the woman who had reared her from the age of five. 'She didn't have a good relationship with our grandfather, did she? His fault, not hers.'

'Hey, hey—be fair now!' Carina was looking more taken aback by the minute. 'I suppose it was *Dad's* fault she couldn't get far enough away from him?' she asked heatedly.

Francesca could see Carina was as upset in her way as she was in hers. 'Look, don't upset yourself, Carrie. It's just that your mother didn't believe it possible to remain locked in a marriage that wasn't working.'

'How can *you* be sure of that?' Carina's matt cheeks were hot with blood. 'You have no insight into relationships. God, you haven't even *had* a real one, have you? You can't count Greg Norbett...or Harry Osbourne,' she added contemptuously.

'Certainly not after you made a play for him.' Francesca surprised herself by making the charge. 'Why did you *do* that? You weren't interested in Harry.'

Carina backed off a notch, touching Francesca's cheek very gently. 'I only did it to make you see what he really was. I didn't want you to get hurt. I've never wanted to see you suffer, Francey. You're still my little lost cousin. I have to look out for you. Harry Osbourne was no good for you.'

'Harry was okay,' Francesca said. 'He was never as close to me as you thought. We weren't lovers. Nothing like that.'

Carina made no effort to conceal her amusement. 'Gosh, are you still a little virgin? I bet you are!' She trilled with laughter that caused heads to turn.

'Maybe, as a Forsyth, I don't fancy the idea of my affairs getting around.'

That appeared to hit the bullseye. 'What does *that* mean?'

Francesca shrugged. 'Nothing, really.' What sense was there in baiting Carina? 'Sadly, not all married couples live happily ever after.'

'Well, *I* plan to.' Carina stared fiercely at her cousin, like a fencing opponent determined on slicing her through. 'I love Bryn. I've always loved him. I was *meant* to have him and I'm going to make certain I do. So don't ever be fool enough to get in my way, cousin.'

Threat came off Carina in waves.

Francesca was all too familiar with the look. Just so had their grandfather looked when he was laying down the law. 'When have I ever done that, Carrie?' she asked quietly. 'We could have been good friends if you'd only given me a chance.'

'Given you a chance?' Carina couldn't have looked more taken aback. 'I've no idea what you're talking about. To my mind we're the best and closest of friends.'

'Surely it's time to face the truth? We're not, Carrie. We might as well stop the pretence.'

Carina was holding her hands so tightly together she might be fearing she would lash out. 'I don't believe this. And on this day of days!'

'Maybe that's the reason. It's the end of an era; the end of the old life. I *wanted* to belong. I wanted us to be more like sisters than cousins. But sadly we were never that.'

Carina's anger suddenly disappeared like a puff of smoke. 'I hate to hear you talk like this, Francey,' she said. 'It makes me feel quite wounded. You obviously have no memory of all the fondness I showed you. What you're saying sounds quite neurotic. I can't help knowing all these years that you've been sick with envy. Don't worry. I forgive you. It's natural enough. But I've always tried to be there for you. I've always tried to protect you from unpleasantness. I shielded you from Gramps. You made him angry, always looking at him with those big tragic eyes. Anyone would think you were accusing him of something.'

Francesca shook her head. 'Nonsense!'

'Not nonsense at all. If I were you, I'd count myself lucky.'

'A lot of the time I do,' Francesca freely admitted. 'Look, Bryn's coming over.'

'He's coming to *me!*' Carina pointed out very sharply, her possessive blue eyes following his progress. 'I dearly need his support.'

'Of course you do.'

The life force that was in Bryn Macallan made him fairly blaze. Both young women felt it. Both were electrified by it.

Francesca made her escape as swiftly as she could. She mightn't know the *whole* truth of Bryn's relationship with her cousin, but she knew enough not to interfere.

If only... If only...

She made the mistake of glancing back, and any tiny hope she might have nourished withered and died. Bryn held an anguished-looking Carrie against his breast, his raven head bent over hers, a shining blonde against the funereal black of his jacket.

Who said unrequited love wasn't hell?

CHAPTER THREE

WHEN Francesca finally made it to the relative sanctuary of her old suite of rooms, she found Dami, the maid, putting a pile of fluffy fresh towels in the *en suite* bathroom, which was almost as big as the living room in Francesca's apartment.

'Is there anything else I can do for you, Ms Forsyth?' Dami asked. She had already unpacked Francesca's things and put them away. 'Would you like tea?'

Francesca glanced out of the window. It was still brilliantly light. 'That would be lovely. Thank you, Dami.' There had been any amount of food and drink downstairs, but she hadn't felt able to touch a thing. The 'mourners', however, standing in groups holding plates and glasses aloft, had availed themselves of the sumptuous spread. It might have been a wedding, not a wake. 'Are you settling in well?' she checked with the maid, who was a fairly recent addition to the staff.

Dami looked shocked to be asked. 'Yes, thank you, miss.' She gave a little nervous bob. 'What kind of tea, please?' Eagerness was visible in every line of her slight body. She began to sound off a list.

It was Francesca's turn to smile. 'Darjeeling will be fine, Dami. Perhaps you could find a sandwich to go with it?' It struck her all of a sudden that she had better have something to keep up her strength.

'Of course, miss,' Dami said, preparing to withdraw. 'Shall I draw a bath for you later?' It was her job to look after Francesca's every need, and she was obviously taking it very seriously.

Francesca shook her head, marvelling that, after a lifetime of it, she still couldn't get used to the Forsyth lifestyle of being waited on hand and foot. Even her grandfather's morning papers had had to be pressed with a warm iron before they were brought to him. 'I'm not sure of my plans, Dami,' she said gently. 'In any case, I can manage, thank you.'

'Yes, miss.' Dami gave another little cork-like bob, then vanished to carry out Francesca's wishes.

After Dami had gone Francesca slipped out of the offending black two-piece suit to which Carina had given the thumbs-down. There was absolutely nothing wrong with it. In fact it was quite elegant. But Carina, she knew, didn't go for the understated. She hung the suit away, then pulled a pair of narrow black linen trousers off the hanger. She had brought a silk blouse to wear with it, silver-grey in colour. Her head was aching so badly she pulled the pins out of the confining knot and then shook her hair free. Immediately she experienced a sense of lightness that seemed to lessen the throbbing pain in her temples. It might be a good idea to wait for Dami to return with her tea before taking any medication. She wasn't used to it. Not that there was a problem with a couple of painkillers.

A few minutes later there was a tap on her door and she went to it, fully expecting to see Dami standing there, either carrying a tray or pushing a trolley. At least she wouldn't have had to come any distance. There was a service elevator, as there had to be in such a mausoleum. Only in the end it wasn't Dami.

Bryn's brilliant black eyes studied her. 'Hi!'

'Hi!' Her heart rose like a bird's. How did one repudiate love? Even when one knew it was paramount to do so?

She yearned for him to lean down and kiss her.

Not her cheek, as was their custom, but her mouth. Wasn't that her most exquisite dream? Only she knew it wasn't good or wise.

'What are you doing here?' She hoped her naked self wasn't there for him to see in her eyes. 'I thought you'd be with Carrie?'

He answered question with question. 'May I come in?'

'Of course.' She stood back to admit him. 'I'll leave the door open. I asked Dami to get me a cup of tea. Would you like one?'

'Dear God, no,' he moaned, walking to the window and looking out over the vast lawn. 'I wanted to see *you.*' He turned around to regard her, catching her in the act of trying to fashion her long lustrous hair into yet another knot. 'Leave it,' he said, his tone more clipped than he'd intended. 'I like seeing your hair down instead of always dragged back.'

Her hands stilled at his command. For that was what it was. A command. 'Gosh, it's not that bad, is it?' she asked wryly.

'Of course not. I'm sorry. I tend to feel a bit strongly about it.'

'Really?' She couldn't have been more surprised. 'So I'll leave it loose, then?'

'Damn it, *yes*. It suits you.' Loose her hair was the very opposite to the sleekness she achieved with her various coils. It sprang away from her face, full of volume. Swirls of hair cascaded sinuously over her shoulders and down her back to her shoulderblades. Yet she obviously considered wearing her hair loose hugely inappropriate on the day of her grandfather's funeral.

'Okay. I get the message. I must remember you don't like my hair pulled back. It's just that I don't like to go down to the will-reading—'

'What has leaving your hair down got to do with the will-reading?' he interrupted. 'It's beautiful hair.'

'I thought you preferred blonde?' It just flew out. She hadn't meant to say it at all. Now she was embarrassed.

'Blonde hair is lovely,' he agreed. 'But it doesn't get the *shine* on it sable hair does.'

'Don't tell Carrie that.'

He gave a half smile. 'Carrie thinks she has the best head of hair in the entire world.'

'Well, she'd have to come close.' Francesca leant over to re-align an ornament. There was the sound of tinkling from the corridor. Silver against china. In the next instant Dami appeared in the open doorway, carrying an elaborate silver tray normally associated with very tall butlers and banquets.

Bryn crossed the room to take the tray from her. 'I'll take that, Dami. It looks too heavy for you.'

'I think maybe a little bit,' Dami admitted, and blushed. 'Shall I fetch another cup?' She looked anxiously from Francesca to Bryn.

'No, that's fine, Dami,' Francesca smiled. 'Mr Macallan doesn't want tea.'

'I can only drink so many cups,' Bryn groaned.

'You would like something else?' the maid asked.

'Nothing, Dami. Thank you.' Francesca shook her head. Even Dami was staring at her flowing mane with what appeared to be outright admiration.

By the time she had closed the door Bryn had poured a cup of tea for her from the silver pot. She had seen it countless times before. It was part of a valuable five-piece Georgian service. The matching lidded sugar bowl was there, and beside it a silver dish with lemon slices. The bone china tea cup and saucer had an exquisite *bleu celeste* border and a gold rim, as did the matching plate, holding an array of delicate triple-layer sandwich fingers, all very elegantly presented.

'Come along,' Bryn said, as though it was his duty to get her to eat. 'I notice you didn't touch a thing downstairs when everyone else was most en-thusiastic. You'd think the whole country was going to be hit by famine in a matter of days.' He glanced back at her. 'Leave your hair alone.'

'Goodness, you're bossy!' she breathed.

'I have to be. I know you grew up thinking your hair had to be tied back in plaits. It was Carrie's golden mane that was always on display. Even Elizabeth knew better than to present you as a foil for her daughter.'

'Oh, hold on!'

'It's true.'

'Okay, it's true. No secrets from you,' she said with a helpless shrug. 'Elizabeth spent a lot of time brushing my hair as a child and telling me how beautiful it was. *"Just like your mother's!"* She always said that, smiling quietly, before hugging me to her with tears in her eyes. She and my mother had become the closest of friends, she said. Growing up in this strange house only Elizabeth affirmed my value. Then she had to make her own escape.'

'Well, the Forsyths tend to stomp on people,' Bryn said, very dryly. 'It took a tremendous amount of guts for your father to get out. He was never forgiven, of course.'

'I used to think *I* bore the brunt of that. The father's sins visited on the daughter?' She hesitated for a moment. 'It's always puzzled me why Elizabeth married Uncle Charles. All right, I know he would have been very handsome—he still is—and a Forsyth with all that money. But he's so…shallow.' She gave a little shamed sob. 'No, I'll take that back. I'm sorry. *Not* shallow. But not a lot to him. Or not a lot that shows.'

Bryn shrugged. 'You know why. Your grandfather drained the life out of him. There's a word for your grandfather, but I can't use it on this particular day. He made his own son feel forever anxious and insecure. He made him feel he would never be good enough to take over the running of the Forsyth Foundation, let alone Titan. Oddly enough, Charles is now acting as though a huge load has been lifted from his shoulders and dropped onto someone else's. Did you notice?' He shot her a laser-like glance. 'He even tried chatting up Elizabeth. He sounded as though he was actually *aching* for her company.'

'I can't think she can be aching for his,' Francesca said sharply, then winced. 'Oh, what would I know? Maybe Uncle Charles knows something the rest of us don't?' She finished off one of the sandwiches, then used the edge of a linen and lace napkin to brush away a crumb.

'He could know the contents of the will,' Bryn mused aloud. 'But it's inconceivable he might be bypassed. Or *is* it?' He spoke as though the thought had just occurred to him.

'What are you saying?' Francesca stared back. 'By tradition Uncle Charles will take over from Grandfather, won't he?'

'Well, we'll soon know.' Bryn deflected her question briskly, an edge of mockery in his tone.

'We?' There was a flicker in her eyes. 'You mean you're staying?' She had thought now that he had brought her home he had come to say goodbye.

'It appears I'm a beneficiary.' He gave a brief laugh that was quite without humour.

'Good Lord! Aren't you wondering what it is?'

Bryn held up a hand. 'A set of golf clubs? He borrowed my grandfather's and never gave them back. Come here, Francey.' He watched her rise gracefully from her chair and walk towards him. 'People do the damnedest thing when it comes to making wills. We all might be in for a few shocks. Even the wicked, like Frank, aren't absolutely sure they won't have to face up to a higher authority. Give an accounting. Face the music. Listen while a long list of sins are read out.'

Her father had been sinned against, Francesca thought. His share of the family fortune had been slashed right back. 'Well, Carrie was very anxious you should stay.' She lifted her eyes to his, aware she was trembling. 'She needs your support.'

'Carrie is well able to look after herself,' he replied, without expression.

'Yes, but we all need a shoulder to cry on from time to time. I couldn't help seeing the two of you together. The way you gathered her to you.' The kind of intimacy she imagined herself and Bryn might share!

'So? What would you have had me do?' he countered, raising a black brow. 'Carrie was looking for comfort. I gave it. All three of us have been locked together since we were kids.'

'I've never felt it was a *triangle*,' Francesca said slowly, hardly able to sustain his concentrated glance. *Until now.*

'Sure about that?' Very gently he lifted a finger and began to twine a silky lock of her hair around it.

The slightest contact; a wild adrenalin rush. 'What are you doing, Bryn?' Her voice quavered, soft and intense. By now he had drawn her face closer, his filled with mesmerising intent.

'Looking at you,' he answered, mildly enough. 'What else? You must be used to it by now. You're very beautiful, Francey, though I see it torments you.' She would have dreaded upstaging Carrie, he knew. Something she could easily have done.

'I'm unsure *why* you're looking at me,' she questioned. 'And with such concentration.'

'Should that make you feel threatened?' He drew back a little, to stare down into her eyes, putting her further off-balance.

Oh, my God... Oh, my God... Oh, my God...

The breath caught in her throat. 'I've never felt *more* threatened.' Her head was beginning to swim.

'Does that happen when I touch you?' A kind of agony was deep in his voice.

Such a change in pace! Such a tremendous build-up in pressure. What was he *doing?* Her heart seemed to be pumping at the base of her throat. Her will giving way under the force of his. 'You are *not* to kiss me, Bryn,' she warned, aware she sounded pathetically frantic. 'If that's what you're planning.' She had been exposed to such a look many times before—desire—but *never* from

Bryn. Yet there seemed no way out. As if it was something he fully intended to do.

Her whole body was locked rigid. All the breath was sucked out of her. How could she resist him? It would take every ounce of her will and self discipline. She knew in her heart of hearts she didn't have enough.

'How do you know I haven't been planning to kiss you for some time?' he challenged her, a burning intensity in his eyes. His hands closed slowly and gently around her throat, a warm, living rope binding her to him.

'Bryn, it makes no sense to experiment.' She tried to free herself to no avail. 'You have no reason to hurt me.'

That appeared to make him angry. '*Hurt you? Would kissing you do that?*' He maintained his hold on her, the air thrumming with electricity.

'You need to consider that possibility.' Even as she argued her position, hot blood was thrashing through her veins. 'It could hardly be worth it.'

'Now, that's where you're wrong,' he said very crisply, his dynamic face all taut planes and angles, his eyes glittering with such dark radiance Francesca was forced to close hers.

Pretend it's make-believe.

How could she, when every nerve was screaming *reality?* Francesca found herself standing perfectly still while his hands slipped over the curve of her shoulders, then he locked a steely arm around her quiescent body.

Sensation was so overwhelming she gasped aloud. She knew she would remember these moments all her life: what it meant to be swept away. But if she allowed herself to go with it, this would be a life-changing moment. An emotional disaster, even. She wasn't equipped to handle disaster.

But what use to fight the tyranny of the senses? His dominant face was bent over her. What could seem absolutely wrong, could also seem absolutely *right.*

He kissed her—not once, but repeatedly, the pleasure blotting out all resistance.

Each kiss was deeper, more seductive, than the last. She could taste the salt of her own tears. 'Bryn, you *mustn't.'* Yet she was going with the moment. It might only happen once. Rapture was flooding her heart and her mind and her body. Filling up every little bit of her, swirling into the deepest recesses. The masks were off!

It was an agony to think of it, but if she didn't stop him soon, she would be totally consumed.

She *had* to end it. There would be no way back. She would never have the life she'd once had again. She *had* to stop him.

She didn't.

Why? She could die for this. Die for it day after day after day…

'Some shall be pardoned, and some punished.'

Who was that? Shakespeare, of course. *Romeo and Juliet* again. Tears ran down her face.

Bryn took them blindly into his mouth, savouring them like nectar. 'Francey, I'm sorry. Don't cry. Please don't cry!' he begged, but the instant he said it his mouth closed on hers again like an all-powerful compulsion. Desire was thundering, smashing through Bryn's defences. Her parted lips bloomed, opened like petals to him.

Just this once. Just this once, Francesca prayed. She couldn't hold back the inexpressibly aching yearning. She couldn't turn away from the sheer splendour. She was truly *alive,* made feverish by the exploration of his tongue, stunned by her own high-spiralling sensuality. The illumination was blinding. She felt ready to give him everything he desired. Thereby flouting every rule by which she had lived.

This is Bryn Macallan.

The warning voice in her head suddenly tolled

loudly, gathering strength as if to deafen her. *Loving him is a danger.*

Hadn't it been drummed into her right from the beginning? He and Carina had been lovers. Could still be, for all she knew. Carina would never give up on Bryn even if Bryn was prepared to. There was a huge difference between her and Carina. *Try to remember it.* Carina was the Forsyth heiress. The perfect partner for Bryn Macallan. Besides, it would break Carina's proud spirit if she were to lose him.

Bryn, sensing her inner turmoil, drew back a moment, looking down at her beautiful face, still in thrall. Her eyes were closed, her long black lashes lying like crescents on her pale golden skin. Slowly he slipped a hand across her face, tracing the fine bone structure.

'I couldn't fight it any more,' he said, an edge to his voice as though his own nerves were jangled. 'The moment was bound to come.'

Her eyes flew open. 'Then we must forget it!' she cried passionately.

His admission had done nothing to calm her troubled heart. The way forward was fraught with dangerous snares. She had revealed herself when she had fought so diligently not to. No other man could affect her like this. No other man could even come close. She had spent so long hiding her true feelings that now she was aghast at what she had done. They had given in to an involuntary urge. That was it. In the stress of the day, they had given way to a passing desire. But did that excuse her? She *knew* how Carrie felt about Bryn. This was *treason.*

'Francey, don't go into a panic.' His voice rasped. He placed his two hands on her delicate shoulders, looking down on her bent head.

'How can I not?' She dared him to doubt it. She had never experienced anything remotely like this. She had never been so aware of the softness of her woman's body against the hardness of a man's, so aware of the expanse of a man's chest, his strong arms enfolding her, his superb fitness, his superior height. It was *thrilling!* But that wasn't all there was to her feeling for Bryn. She had enormous respect for him. She didn't want that to change. She had always turned to him for support. As a child; as an adult. Still she was afraid. If Bryn wanted her even for a brief moment there was much to be afraid of. In the heat of the moment both of them had taken a great step into the unknown.

'Francey, I'm sorry. I've obviously upset you.' He could see her anguish.

'There's no future in this, Bryn,' she pleaded. 'You know that. More likely there will be consequences.'

'Don't be ridiculous!' He cut her off more harshly than he knew. 'You sound like you might never be seen again.'

'Like Gulla Nolan?' The name tumbled from her lips. What mysterious force had prompted her to mention *him?* And why now?

A darkness descended on Bryn's face. 'Whatever made you bring up Gulla Nolan?'

'God knows.' She found the strength to break away. 'I can't pretend *I* do. His name just came into my mind.' Her eyes were shimmering like silver lakes. 'The last thing I want, Bryn, is to threaten our friendship. It means everything to me.'

His handsome features tightened. 'Francey, I'm much *more* than your friend.'

She rounded on him. 'So don't break my heart. Don't break Carrie's heart. I'm speaking for both of us.'

His reply carried swift condemnation. 'I guess that means you don't want to break out of your safe little hidey-hole?'

She reacted as if he had slapped her. Her cheeks

flushed. 'You might say that. I have to forget what's happened here, Bryn. I'm sure you will too. It's an odd day all round. There's so much at stake.'

'Like what?' he asked sharply, staring at her with what she thought was a lick of contempt.

She reacted by throwing up helpless hands. 'You know the answer to that. What *is* it you want from me? *Really?*' Tears gathered again behind her eyes. 'I'll never forgive you if you tell me those kisses meant nothing.' Could romantic dreams possibly become romantic nightmares?

The answer was yes.

'I wasn't the only one who lost my head, Francey,' he told her bluntly. 'If that's what you're convinced it was. I always knew there was a lot of passion behind the Madonna façade.'

'Well, I'm not proud of myself,' she uttered emotionally. 'You're a very sensual man, Bryn. I admit I lost my head. But it's not as though you intend to make a practice of it.' What she had most ardently desired was now worrying the life out of her. But such was her perilous world. The world of the Forsyths and the Macallans. Enough money and power to act any way they liked. Great wealth created impregnable cocoons. Carina would not be mocked.

'I'll be fighting not to for a while,' he told her, bitterly sardonic. 'But let's leave it there, shall we?' He turned purposefully towards the door, tall and commanding. 'This conversation is going nowhere.'

'Because it *can't*.'

His black eyes were full of scorn. 'So you're *still* the little girl afraid to step out of her cousin's shadow?'

She reacted with spirit, even though she could see the smouldering anger in his eyes. 'That's a brutal thing to say, Bryn.'

His laugh cut into her deeply. 'The truth often is. But I won't press it further. Not today, anyway. But it's high time you took up a full life and started slaying your dragons, Francey. You're the best and the brightest of the Forsyths. Wake up to it.'

It was a pep talk he obviously thought she was badly in need of. She wrapped her arms around herself protectively. 'I'm sorry, Bryn. I'm sorry we got into this.'

'It didn't feel like you were sorry when you were in my arms,' he pointed out, so cuttingly she flushed. 'Anyway, forget it. What's done *is* done.'

'I'm sorry,' she repeated. She couldn't bear to see him walk away in anger. She made a huge effort to change the subject before he left. 'Can you tell me something before you go? Please? Something I've always wondered about. That old story of Gulla Nolan...the way he disappeared without trace.'

Bryn froze in his tracks. Hadn't he mulled over the old mystery for years? How strange Francey should bring it up now. But then that sort of thing often happened with Francey. Over the years she had said many things to catch him off guard and cause him to re-think. 'What is there to tell? No one knows anything. A thorough investigation was carried out. The tribal people on and around the station were questioned.'

'Maybe they did know something but feared to speak out.' She looked back at him, huge-eyed. 'Who would have believed them anyway? Things being what they were—still are—an aboriginal's word against the findings of Sir Francis Forsyth? Unthinkable! They hated him with a passion. Maybe they even put a curse on him and his family. My family. My parents—' She broke off, knowing she was deeply overwrought.

He retraced his steps. 'No, Francey, *no!*' He made no further attempt to touch her. 'Don't even go there,' he warned. 'My grandfather had Gulla's disappearance investigated. He shared a real bond with Gulla. But in the end no one knew anything. Gulla went on extended binges. That in itself was a danger. His disappearance is just another bush legend.'

'You don't really believe that,' she said. 'I can hear it in your voice. You're just saying it to make me feel better. Even if he had died out there and the dingoes had taken his body the bones would have been found, traces of his clothing.'

Resolutely he turned on his heel, ignoring the dull roaring in his ears. 'We should go downstairs.'

'You mean before Carina comes up?' Her voice shook.

'Neither of us should put it past her.' His tone was openly ironic. 'Look, Francey, I don't want you walking around in a state of dread. I won't even look sideways at you if you don't want it.'

'Don't look at me *at all* might be better.'

He gave a hard, impatient laugh. 'I can't go so far as to promise that. So don't expect it. Let's just take it one day at a time, shall we? And do try to remember I'm *not* a married man. Not engaged either, last time I checked.'

* * *

Douglas McFadden, distinguished senior partner of McFadden, Mallory & Crawford, the Forsyth family solicitors, was seated behind the late Sir Francis Forsyth's massive, rather bizarre mahogany desk in the study. The desk was lavishly decorated with ormolu mounts and lions' feet, the gilded claws extended. Francesca had been truly frightened of those claws as a small child.

Like the rest of the mansion, the ballroom-sized study was hugely over the top. A life-size portrait of Sir Francis in his prime—some seven feet tall and almost as wide, its colours enriched by the overhead light—hung centre stage on the wall behind the desk. It said a great deal for her grandfather—undeniably a strikingly handsome man, if not with the look of distinction the Macallans had in abundance—that the portrait was able to dominate such an impressive room. The artist was quite famous, and he had captured her grandfather's *innerness,* Francesca thought. The man behind the mask. Francesca found herself looking away from those piercing, somehow *gloating* blue eyes.

The beneficiaries, some fourteen in all, looked suitably sober. With the exception of Bryn they were all Forsyths, like herself: some the offspring of her grandfather's two younger sisters, Ruth and Regina, who wisely lived very private lives, well out of their brother's orbit. Four of the grandsons, however, worked for Titan. Sir Francis himself had recruited them, as some sort of gesture towards 'family'. They did their best—they were clever, highly educated—but they could never hope to measure up to Bryn Macallan in any department. At least one of them—James Forsyth-Somerville—knew it. Bryn Macallan was his hero.

Bryn, the outsider, sat as calm and relaxed as though they were all attending a lecture to be given by some university don. Possible topic: was Shakespeare the real author of his plays? Or was it much more likely to have been the brilliant and aristocratic Francis Bacon, or even Edward De Vere? Anyway, it was a talk Bryn appeared to be looking forward to. He sat wedged—the delectable filling in a sandwich—between herself and Carina. The two Forsyth heiresses. She had to recognise she was that. Much as she had sought to remain in the background, she *was* an heiress—a Forsyth, like it or not.

'I don't care where the hell you sit, as long as Bryn is with me!' Carina had snapped at her as they had entered the study, lined with a million beauti-fully bound books her grandfather had never read.

Bryn, however, had taken his place on Francesca's right. 'Okay, I hope?' he'd asked with faint mockery, causing Carina, who had seated herself dead centre, directly in front of the desk, and had patted the seat beside her, indicating for Bryn to take it, to jump up and grab the other chair, pure venom in her eyes.

In the end everyone was arranged in a two-tiered semicircle in front of the huge mahogany desk. It was difficult to believe Sir Francis was dead. One of the great-nephews, Stephen, kept looking behind him, as though expecting Sir Francis's ghost to walk right through the heavy closed door.

Francesca had noticed her uncle Charles had poured himself a stiff whisky before positioning himself to one side, as though instead of being her grandfather's only surviving son and heir he didn't think he would figure much in the will. How very odd!

A quick glance at Bryn confirmed it. 'Could be a rocky ride!' he murmured, just beneath his breath. He looked tremendously switched on. Ready for the performance to begin.

The elder of Sir Frank's two sisters, Ruth,

choked off a little sob, probably thinking there was still time to show a little grief. She hadn't been able to manage it up to date. Carina, however, wasn't impressed by the display. She swung about to frown at her great-aunt. 'For God's sake, not *now!*'

Ruth leaned towards her, murmuring a falsehood. 'But I'm missing him so!'

'Rubbish! You haven't so much as spoken to him for months,' Carina flashed back, before turning to address the always dapper solicitor, with his full head of snow-white hair of which he was justifiably proud. 'Well, what are we waiting for, Douglas? Read it out.'

Bryn leaned in towards Francesca, his voice low. 'A command—and a very terse one at that! Frank couldn't have done better.'

Francesca prayed fervently there wouldn't be more outbursts from Carina. If their grandfather had been a tiger, Carina was a tigress in the making.

As though in agreement, Charles Forsyth sank back heavily in his chair. The room stank of danger! Ruth gave another hastily muffled moan. She too was unnerved by the fact that her great-niece had turned into what looked very much like the female version of her late brother. Frank might have come back from wherever he had gone.

Francesca stole another glance at Bryn, thinking that in some strange way they were acting very much like a pair of conspirators. Bryn reacted by raising his brows slightly, his smile laced with black humour. He was inoculated against Carina's outbursts.

Francesca sat quiet as a nun, pale as an ivory rose, her elegant long legs to one side, and her head, with her hair in a sort of Gibson Girl loose arrangement, inclined to the other, showing off her swan's neck and the delicate strength of her clean jawline. She might have been the subject of a painting herself, Bryn thought. A study of a beautiful, *isolated* young woman. He vowed to himself that state of affairs wasn't going to continue. The sleeping princess had to wake up.

Douglas McFadden responded impassively to Carina's rudeness. He had had half a lifetime of it from Sir Francis. 'Very well, Carina,' he said obligingly, picking up his gold-rimmed glasses. He did, however, take his time to settle them on his beak of a nose. Once done, he appeared to take a deep breath, then launched into the reading of the last will and testament of Sir Francis Gerard Oswald Forsyth...

Already Francesca had begun to panic. She desperately wanted it all over. Great wealth ruined people. She had seen it with her own eyes. But none of them, with the exception of Charles Forsyth, was prepared for what was to come.

It was Carina who tempestuously brought proceedings to a halt.

'It *can't* be true!' She catapulted out of her chair, sending it crashing to the floor. Her blonde hair flew around her visibly blanched face. Her furious blue eyes lashed the solicitor. 'What kind of bloody lunacy is this?' she shouted, her voice loud enough to shock the profoundly deaf. Her arms flailed wildly in the air, causing her copious eighteen carat gold bracelets to out-jangle a brass band.

'Carrie…Carrie.' Charles Forsyth very belatedly tried his hand at remonstrating with his headstrong daughter, while the great-aunts moved their chairs closer together, in case things got so bad they might have to cling to each other for support. Their menfolk stared steadily at the Persian rug, their faces varying shades of red.

Bryn moved smoothly to pick up Carina's chair, setting it right. 'Why don't you sit down again, Carrie?' He placed a kindly restraining hand on her shoulder. He didn't appear at all shocked by Carina's outburst, Francesca noticed. Indeed, he was looking about him, as though deciding on the next object Carina might send toppling.

'You're supposed to be here to support me, Bryn!' she protested, not sparing a glance in her father's direction. She ignored him. As she would from that day forward. Nothing her father said from now on would hold much value for her.

'Please. Sit down,' Bryn advised, bringing his powerful influence to bear.

Carina obeyed. 'Just *when* did Gramps make such a will?' she cried out the moment she was seated. 'I *know* what was in his will—the real will—and it surely wasn't this! This stinks to high heaven of conspiracy.'

Douglas McFadden pursed his lips and looked profoundly displeased. 'I beg your pardon, Carina.'

'Carrie…Carrie,' Charles Forsyth bleated. His fair handsome face was ruddy with distress. 'It's all in order, I assure you.'

Carina's blazing blue eyes narrowed to slits. 'You *knew* about this, Dad? What kind of a fool *are* you? You're the great *loser!* You've been cut out, and you look like you're accepting it. Gramps has publicly dismissed and humiliated you. *You* are the rightful heir. *You* administer the Forsyth Foundation. You *have* to fight this. By my reckoning you'll win.'

'Don't bet on that.' Bryn sent her a lancing glance.

'But… But…' Carina actually sputtered, looked fearfully taken aback.

'I'm not fighting anything, Carina,' Charles Forsyth told her quietly, but with surprising finality. 'I'm very happy with my lot.'

'Which is a lot *indeed*,' Bryn murmured. Maybe Charles would become a better man, a more self-confident man, without his father forever glowering over his shoulder, stripping him of any hope of self-esteem.

Carina glared her contempt for her father. 'Why would you be happy?' she cried, turning into the daughter from hell right in front of his glazed eyes. 'Gramps was right about you. You don't fire on all cylinders. Don't you *understand* what's happened here? You don't even look upset. You've been treated disgracefully. *I've* been treated disgracefully.'

'You've been left a great fortune, Carrie,' Bryn pointed out. 'Give yourself a moment to let that sink in.'

She blushed hotly. 'Do you *mind?* We've been passed over.'

'Not really, Carrie. What *more* do you want?' her father added, grateful for Bryn's intervention.

'A damned sight more than you seem to think.' Carina swung her blonde head back to face the solicitor. 'You ought to be disbarred, McFadden. You're as big a fool as Dad.'

The great-aunts gasped. They had never heard anything so nasty. And to dear Douglas!

'I really don't have to listen to this, Carina.' Douglas McFadden, veteran of countless highly volatile will-readings, spoke in a perfectly even tone. 'I have carried out your late grandfather's instruction to the letter. It was his wish that his granddaughter, Francesca Elizabeth Mary Forsyth, should control the Forsyth Foundation. I would remind you, as Bryn has tried to do, that your late grandfather knew *exactly* what he was doing.'

'He couldn't have!' Carina was just barely resisting the violent urge to scream. 'Gramps had no great love for Francesca. Hell, most of the time he ignored her.'

'Perhaps he knew things about *you,* Carrie, that made him act like that?' Charles Forsyth suggested, in a voice that bore overtones of guilt.

'That's the trouble with you, Dad—'

Once again Bryn put out a restraining hand. 'There's more to be read, Carrie. Why don't you let Douglas get on with it?'

'I'd like to,' Douglas McFadden said, peering over the top of his spectacles. 'I really would. As Sir Francis has clearly stated, he deeply regretted falling out with his late son Lionel, Francesca's father. He may not have shown the depth of his regret, but he spoke to me many times about it. It was very much on his mind. He trusted me as his friend and adviser—especially after the loss of his closest lifelong friend Sir Theo.' The solicitor inclined his head respectfully in Bryn's direction. 'Sir Theo's much loved grandson is here today, and is also a beneficiary. I would like to point out that Francesca was at the very top of the law graduates of her year—no mean feat—though she has chosen art as her career. A *successful* career, I might add.'

Again Carina projected her naturally loud voice, as though the solicitor was in desperate need of a hearing aid. 'Since when were *you* an authority on the kind of things Francesca does, Douglas?' she challenged him. 'All that Dreamtime stuff.'

Bryn turned on her eyes that had grown daunting, with a downward cast to his beautifully curved lips. 'If I were you I'd be a little bit worried about heaping ridicule on the Dreamtime, Carrie. There could be some danger in that. And actually, Douglas is a recognised art connoisseur, with a fine collection.'

'That Gramps paid for,' Carina bit off. 'But not Francey's own stuff. I think it's pitiful.'

'Then we can all rest assured that it's good,' Bryn returned suavely, forcing Carina to swallow hard.

Oh, my Lord! Francesca furtively pressed Bryn's jacketed arm, trying to signal him to stop. It was abundantly clear that Carrie was bitterly resenting Bryn's defence of her.

Douglas McFadden judged it time to intervene. 'What conversations Sir Francis and others *have* had with Francesca—who *was* named after her grandfather—led him to believe she has a very fine mind. Her viewpoint *counted,* in his opinion. He was convinced she had inherited *his* and her own father's head for business.'

'And you expect us to *believe* this?' Carina ground out the words with difficulty, her jaw was so locked on its hinges. 'Francesca has a fine mind and *I* don't?'

'Of course you do, Carina.' Douglas McFadden gave her a deeply conciliatory look. 'But, well…you never did take much interest… I mean…' Unusually for him, he began to stammer, but Carina Forsyth in full flight was not a pretty sight. She had broken through all normal control. Which didn't really surprise him after all.

To prove it, Carina's voice rose meteorically. 'Gramps wasn't happy about women in business, Douglas. You know that. Tell him, Bryn.' She appealed to the still seated Bryn. He was unmoving, yet he still exuded energy and a blazing intensity. 'Don't just bloody sit there mocking us all. Gramps was very proud of me the way I am. I'm the most photographed woman in the country, and certainly the best-looking and the best dressed. Now *this!* Why should *one* person have control? And Francesca, at that! She has absolutely no *right.*' She flashed her cousin a look of furious anger and betrayal, as though Francesca had spent years working on their grand-father behind the scenes.

'She *is* a Forsyth,' Bryn pointed out provocatively.

It caught Carina blindside. 'Oh, *Bryn!*' She would devour the woman who took Bryn away from her.

'It has come as a shock to you, Carina. I can see that.' Douglas McFadden spoke with empathy in his voice. 'But Sir Francis gave long and careful thought to this. As your father and Bryn have pointed out, you have been left a great fortune. You were considered at one time...but your grandfather had to make a final decision. Charles had indicated he feared the heavy responsibilities. Isn't that so, Charles? Your grandfather took note. *You,* as of now, are one of the richest women in the country, Carina—free to do anything you want for as long as you want. But in the end Sir Francis came to believe Francesca was the best person in the family to head up the Foundation. She's clever. She gets on well with people from all walks of life. She is highly principled. She knows what duty is all about, and the burden of responsibilities that come with great wealth. She is her father's daughter, and she will have her advisers around her. Her grandfather firmly believed she would have the wisdom to *listen* to what they have to say and take it on board. He believed she has the capacity to properly evaluate the thousands of requests the Forsyth Foundation receives annually. Furthermore, he believed she would carry out his wishes to the letter. He may not have been the greatest of philanthropists during his lifetime—'

Many would have said *miserly,* Bryn thought.

'—as was his closest friend and partner Sir Theo, but he wished for things to be different in the future. He was, in fact, very proud of the way Francesca has set about making something of herself. The way she's using her own money to fund the promotion of aboriginal art. Very proud indeed. Francesca is a compassionate young woman. Compassion is what the Foundation needs when it comes to prioritising future grants.'

Not everyone agreed. 'Francey? But she's only a baby. This sounds like a disaster!' A scandalised Ruth whispered to her shellshocked sister behind her hand. 'What will people think?'

'Yes, what *will* people think?' Carina, who had the hearing of a nocturnal bat, swung her blonde head over her shoulder to stare down her flustered great-aunts. 'God knows what you two will get. That's if anything is left.'

Bryn, every nerve-ending in his body sensitised to Francesca's reactions, extended the hand that had been hanging loosely at his side. Francesca grasped it for dear life. It couldn't have been more obvious that she was stunned by all she had heard. Perhaps most of all the fact her grandfather had been *proud* of her.

To confirm it, Francesca took a deep, shaky breath. Her grandfather had always acted as if she barely existed for him. Now *this!* This was a whole new dynamic. Couldn't he have said just *once* he was proud of her? Given her a clue? She would only have needed him to say it *once.*

Francesca, I'm proud of you!

She could have lived on it for years.

Carina, so intent on conveying to her great-aunts the shocking injustice of it all, missed the significant linking of hands. Instead she gave a whooping hysterical laugh. 'Gramps must have been off his rocker!' she hooted, turning back to the solicitor. 'Whoever made that will wasn't the real Gramps at all. More like some pathetic old guy whose mind was starting to wander. What does he want her to do, anyway? *Give* it all away? I warn you right now, Francesca will do that—*big-time!* There'll be no fortune left. She's a genuine bleeding heart!' She was alight with self-righteous rage. 'I don't want to hear another word of this. Gramps *adored* me, yet he has given Francey the whip hand over me. Forget Dad. He's gutless. He only wants *out!*'

Francesca's beautiful skin flushed with dismay. 'Uncle Charles—Carrie—I'm not happy about any of this,' she said, appealing to each one in turn. 'I'm as shocked as you are.'

'Believe that and you'll believe anything!' Carina was laughing full-on, with scathing cynicism.

'But, Carrie, it's *true*. I'd be happy to give it all back to you.'

She was conscious that Bryn had pressed her hand hard, no doubt telling her to shut up.

'And we'll be happy to take it,' Carina snapped back. 'You little *Judas!*'

Bryn's resonant voice suddenly boomed, stopping even Carina in her tracks. 'Carrie, that's enough. Francey has no need to explain herself or make any apology to anyone,' he said in a hard, disgusted tone. 'You can see how shocked she is. She had no idea. I suggest we allow Douglas to finish the reading. You can carry on *after* that, if you like. The rest of us can beat a retreat.'

'You mean you're taking Francey's side over mine?' For a moment Carina looked utterly confused. 'You really think I'm going to shut up and take this, Bryn? What the hell—?' She broke off, finally registering the linked hands—one so darkly tanned, the other the smoothest pale gold. 'Well, well, well,' she snarled, now in a white-hot rage. 'What have we got here?'

'You've got *me* offering *Francey* support,' Bryn replied without a moment's hesitation.

This put Carina into an ecstasy of jealousy and hate. 'Let go of the conniving little bitch's hand.'

It was obvious Bryn wasn't going to let that slide. His expression turned so daunting the very air in the room froze. 'I think you've reached the point where you'd do best to shut up, Carrie,' he warned, brilliant eyes aglitter.

But Carina was too far gone. 'Can I trust you, Bryn. *Can* I?' Her blue eyes raked his dynamic face. 'You haven't hatched a little plan or anything?'

'You want someone to trust, Carrie, you'd better find a puppy,' he returned with biting humour.

The battle lines had been drawn. The enemy was in plain view.

It was a total nightmare, Francesca thought. The worst possible disaster. Yet through it all Bryn continued to keep hold of her hand.

'Going to turn our attention to Francey now, are we?' Carina challenged him with great bitterness. 'You'd do anything to get control of Titan. We all know that. You'd even take up with Francey and abandon me. You swore you loved me. You swore when the time was right we'd get married.'

Bryn uttered a single word. 'Delusional.'

How easy it is to sow the seeds of doubt, Francesca thought. She thought of those long passionate kisses Bryn had given her. How could Bryn, of all people, do a thing like that when he had made a promise to Carina? It *wasn't* Bryn. It didn't fit anything she knew about him. Nevertheless, she very quietly withdrew her hand from his, before Carina took it into her head to spring at her like a jungle cat. Could it be possible Bryn was deliberately provoking Carina?

A charged atmosphere surrounded them both. Carina, mercifully, stayed in place, while Bryn rose to his impressive height, as though standing guard over the more vulnerable Francesca.

'Am I?' Carina cried. 'Delusional? Why would I be? You *know* what we talked about.' She transferred her burning blue gaze to her cousin. 'Don't let him fool you. Or has he started to already? He's as devious as they come. The master manipulator. Gramps always said that. He warned me we always had to be on our guard around Bryn. I know he was talking to you in your room, Francesca. The maid told me.'

'Poor thing!' Bryn cut in derisively. 'I bet it was more like an interrogation.'

'Carrie, please stop,' Charles Forsyth said with

surprising authority. 'You too, Bryn. We really don't need all these personal matters to be aired here. Douglas needs to proceed.'

'Of course he does!' Carina hissed. 'But I'll have my say if I want. This *is* my home.'

'*My* home,' her father corrected her, in a voice no one had ever heard him use with her before. This was his princess. Or at least she had been, until she had started making it very plain she thought her father thoroughly deserved to be overthrown.

Oddly, Carina looked tremendously shocked. She blinked. 'So you want me out?' She clenched her hands in front of her breast, as though at any moment her father might have one of the servants pitch her out onto the street. She realised in a rare moment of self-evaluation that any one of them would be pleased to.

'Don't be absurd, Carina,' her father answered, torn between parental loyalty and pity. 'Of course this is your home.'

'I should damned well think so.' Carina returned fire; she was nothing if not resilient. 'So what does *he* get out of it?' She resumed her seat, pointing an accusing finger at Bryn, who was now sitting in an elegant slouch, his expression quite unreadable. 'Let's hear it. More shares in Titan?

The Macallans already own twenty-three percent of the company.' The Forsyths had the majority shareholding in the multi-billion-dollar corporation; something that had happened only after Sir Francis had succeeded the late Sir Theo Macallan and became Chairman and CEO.

'I'll continue now to read out Sir Francis's wishes.' The solicitor consulted the impressive-looking legal document. 'Ah, y-e-e-s,' he said slowly. 'Bryn Barrington Theodore Macallan, in recognition of his own outstanding abilities and his valuable contributions to the ever-escalating success of Titan, and in memory of my great affection and admiration for his late grandfather, my lifelong friend, Sir Theodore Macallan—'

'Get on with it, Douglas,' Carina barked, in a frenzy of impatience.

Douglas McFadden's pale grey eyes narrowed, but he spoke at the same measured pace. 'Bryn Macallan inherits a fifty percent share in Sir Francis's pastoral empire, its flagship being Daramba. Francesca inherits the other fifty percent on the understanding that Bryn is in sole charge of the business end of the enterprise. Evidently Sir Francis believed Francesca would be fully occupied elsewhere, whilst Bryn was the best man to handle an extra job. Charles had already indicated to his father he had little interest in the pastoral side of things. Rule number one with Sir Francis was always, Who is the best person to handle the job?'

Bryn, who after all these years among the Forsyths had thought himself impervious to shock, felt winded. It was as if he had received a violent blow to the solar plexus. He swallowed on the startled oath that was stuck somewhere in his throat. He had been way off the mark in expecting some token bequest. Maybe his grandfather's golf clubs back. This was astounding news—or maybe Frank's last-ditch attempt to get into heaven? He turned his head to gauge Francesca's reaction. She was trembling with emotion, as well she might be. Her eyes were huge with distress, the pearly grey of her blouse further brightening their silver lustre. In all probability she was retreating once more into her protective shell.

Carina had well and truly brought her fierce jealousy out into the open. Damn her lies! Marriage was a word he'd never mentioned. Let alone thought about. That went for the L word as well. What he and Carina had had for a short time was sex—which had turned out to be a terrible mistake. Not that he had taken advantage of an innocent young virgin. Carina had a head start on just about everyone in that department. A free spirit, or so she called herself—even in those days. But he knew as well as anyone: throw enough mud and some was bound to stick. The undermining would continue. He had to be prepared for it. Carina, like her grandfather before her, would never let up. As for his bequest? Given a moment or two to reflect, he knew what Francis Forsyth had ripped off from the Macallans over the years would pay for this share of Forsyth Pastoral Holdings many times over.

Francis Forsyth had evidently believed in a Supreme Being after all. Maybe even in meeting up with Sir Theo and old Gulla again. Highly unlikely. Their destinations would be poles apart.

CHAPTER FOUR

'ALL I'm saying is, give yourself time for it to sink in,' Bryn advised. He had accompanied the stunned and visibly upset Francesca back to her apartment, where at least she thought she would be safe.

'This is a disaster, Bryn. You know it is.' She led the way into the living room, switching on lights as she went.

When she had left here this morning she had never dreamed what the day would bring: the massive upheavals, the responsibilities that were waiting to claim her. If she *wanted* them. She wasn't at all sure she needed a lifetime of being in the front line. Strangely enough, she thought she *could* make a better fist of handling the Foundation than either her grandfather or her uncle. But there were other huge responsibilities. She tried to calm herself with the thought that she would have first-class people around her to advise and guide her. She could afford to hire the best minds. Douglas McFadden had given her the definite impression he thought she was up to the task. And Bryn had appeared to welcome it. No one's opinion was more important to her than Bryn's.

Now he spoke in a clipped voice, a decided edginess about him. 'I know nothing of the kind, Francey. You're very young to take on so much, but age isn't an issue like it used to be. Youth can be a big advantage. Fresh ideas. Seniority has gone by the board. It's a case of the best person for the job. You're it. Whatever else Frank was, he was no fool. He wanted to keep the Forsyth fortune intact, not frittered away.'

Such a clever, complex man was Bryn. Macallan to her Forsyth; Montague to Capulet. Warring families. Since the death of Bryn's grandfather hadn't that been the case? Even if the war had been largely waged underground? Bryn followed her, removing his beautifully tailored black jacket, finely pin-striped, before throwing it over the back of an armchair. Then he unbuttoned the collar of his white shirt and yanked down his black tie as if it were choking him. 'It's one hell of a shock, I know. But think about it. Charles wants out. No problem there. I thought he was very reasonable about the whole thing. He never wanted a career in business in the first place. He was forced into it. Now he's his own man, or near enough. There's no immutable law of nature that says great talent has to be passed down to the next generation. Charles has no head for business. Your father, though the younger brother, was the logical heir. Sir Frank, even if he did his level best not to show it, was shattered when your father was killed. It seems he had expected them to make up. A tragedy all round.'

Her own assessment. Francesca sank dazedly into the comfort of one of the custom-made sofas covered in cream silk. She'd had a whole range of silk cushions made—gold, orange, imperial yellow, bronze and a deep turquoise—to pick up the colours in the exquisite eighteenth-century six-panel lacquered screen mounted on the wall. The screen had belonged to her parents, as did so many pieces of the furniture, paintings and objets d'art, a mix of classical European and Asian, in the apartment. They had been in storage all these years from the old house. What she had done, in effect, was wrap herself around with her own family even if they had gone and left her.

'Yes,' she agreed soberly, 'a tragedy.'

e giant enterprise. Certain men—men like her randfather and Bryn—could successfully juggle ny number of companies without once dropping he ball or losing sight of their objectives. Bryn would probably transform Forsyth Pastoral Holdings, which she knew in recent years had suffered sharply reduced profits and too many changes in management.

'If we're going to be charitable, and I suppose we might find it in our hearts to be after what today has brought, he *has,*' Bryn replied wryly. 'If you ask me, Charles wants to get back with Elizabeth.'

The same bizarre thought had occurred to Francesca. 'Then he has his work cut out for him,' she said. 'Just as Grandfather bullied him, he tried to bully Aunt Elizabeth. Only Carrie was safe.'

'Safe?' One of Bryn's black brows shot up. 'Carrie was a little dictator from the day she was born.'

Another sharp comment from Bryn? 'Well, she must have changed a lot after I arrived.' Francesca looked back on the past. 'I remember her as being very *contained,* even secretive.'

'Oh, she's that!' Bryn agreed, then markedly changed the subject, impatient with more talk of Carina. 'God, I could knock back a Scotch!' He heaved a sigh.

'Are you okay?' He studied her intently. th
lost all colour.' In the space of a single g
willowy slenderness now bordered on the a
Francesca fascinated him. She had always s t
to him quite simply unique.

'I will be when my mind clears and my b
starts flowing again.' She rested her head bac
wish my father were still here.'

How well Bryn understood that, having be
cruelly robbed of his own parent. 'Misfortune (
both our houses,' he said grimly. '*Your* fathe
could handle what was too difficult and too big fo
Charles. Not good for Charles's ego. Their mother
was the only one who was kind to Charles.' He
didn't mention Charles's mother, or all the women
Sir Francis, confirmed widower, had had in his life
since the demise of his wife without elevating a
single one of them to the stature of second wife.
Too canny to be caught with a huge settlement if
a second marriage fell through.

'So in his way Uncle Charles has had a sad life.'
She looked up at Bryn—the man who had brought
her so throbbingly alive; the man her own grandfather had made partner in his pastoral empire.
Her grandfather must have seen Bryn was far and
away the best person to take over the running of

'Please, help yourself.' She waved a listless arm. 'I don't seem able to get up.'

'Why would you? You're winded, like me. Can I get you something?' he asked, moving towards a drinks trolley that held an array of spirits in crystal decanters; whisky, brandy, bourbon, several colourful bottles of liqueur, all at the ready for Francesca's guests.

'Glass of white wine,' she said, not really caring one way or the other. 'There's a bottle of Sauvignon Blanc in the fridge. You'll have to open it.'

He was back within moments, handing her a glass. She took it, savouring the fresh, fruity bouquet before allowing herself a long sip. 'No point in saying cheers, though most people would think I had a great deal to cheer about. Little do they know!'

'We were both born into a world of privilege, Francey,' Bryn said, taking a good pull on the single malt and letting it slide down his throat. 'Responsibilities and obligations go along with that. For us, anyway.' He didn't join her on the sofa, but took a seat in a parcel-gilt walnut antique armchair that was covered in a splendid petit-point. The bright colours stood out in high relief against his darkness—the black eyes and the black hair, the skin darkly tanned from the time he spent sailing as much as his hectic schedule would allow. It comforted her to see him sitting there, like some medieval prince. The armchair was one of a pair her parents had bought in Paris on their very last trip there.

'Carina may not have got what she confidently expected, but she's been left a very rich woman in her own right. Boy, wasn't she a shocker, telling poor old Douglas off? Once or twice she even made me laugh. All those war whoops she kept giving. When she was a kid her grandfather gave her full permission to disregard her mother's efforts to mould her. Your grandfather was very pleased she was showing some "spirit", as he thought of it. Showed she took after him and not her father. Whatever you remember, you must realise Carina was a very spoilt little girl? Now she's a spoilt young woman, determined on running amok. Did you notice Ruth's husband, a distinguished medical scientist? He spent the time trying to look like he wasn't there at all. And Regina's very agreeable husband—I like him— was afraid to speak in case he got told to stay out of it. I don't think any one of them smiled, even when they found out they were leaving considerably better off than when they'd arrived. None of them is going begging in the first place; in fact, there's quite a few hundred million between them.'

'They were all looking very warily at me, I noticed,' Francesca commented wryly. 'Even James—and I thought he liked me.'

'He more than *likes* you,' Bryn pointed out dryly, amused when she didn't appear to hear, or care if she did. Poor old James!

'No one had the faintest idea what Grandfather intended.'

'Charles knew,' Bryn said. 'He sat to one side, knowing he wouldn't be named as his father's heir as everyone expected. As for the rest of us! Nobody knows what tomorrow might bring.'

'Did *you* know?' she found herself asking, realising how desperately she needed that vital piece of information.

His dark head shot up, a flash of anger like summer lightning in his eyes. 'Francey, you *can't* be suggesting I knew in advance about the will and what your grandfather intended for you?'

'Just a question,' she said lamely, and then looked away, unable to sustain that concentrated gaze.

'Not *just a question* at all,' he fired back. 'Let me put it bluntly. Do you or do you not trust me?' He spoke as if her trust or lack of it was crucial to their friendship.

'I wonder you should ask,' she evaded, suddenly beset by myriad doubts.

'But *you* asked, and I want to know.' He wasn't letting her off the hook. 'Did you consider even for a single moment that I knew the contents of your grandfather's will and didn't tell you?'

She could feel her whole body going enormously weak. At that moment she lacked the capacity to deny it. 'I won't lie to you, Bryn. I don't want any lies or evasions between us. It did cross my mind, but for *less* than a moment. You *are* a Macallan.'

'Is that it?' he asked ironically. 'I'm a Macallan, and therefore not to be trusted?'

She paused before speaking. 'Bryn, I would trust you with my life. I *owe* you my life. But I also know of the conflicts that lie at your heart. You won't discuss them with me, even when I ask what's at the root of the enmity I've so easily divined. You, Lady Macallan and Annette, your mother, both of whom I love and respect, all considered my grandfather to have been a scoundrel.'

Bryn tossed back the rest of his drink, then moved back to the drinks trolley for a refill. 'God, what a day! *Most* people thought Frank a great rogue, Francey.' He expelled a long breath. 'For all the things he did to anyone who opposed him, and to competitors in business, be they so-called friends or colleagues. He could have been condemned a thousand times over.'

'But it's far more than that with you. It's deeply personal. I know you won't rest until you're CEO of Titan.'

He turned back to her, his whole persona on high alert. He had such a range of expressions, she thought. One minute daunting, the next the most beautiful smile in the world, and then, when he was engrossed in something he found interesting or beautiful, his striking face turned vividly expressive. At certain times too, like now, he had a look of what the French would call *hauteur.* It wasn't arrogance. Bryn wasn't arrogant—unless it was the unconscious arrogance of achievement.

'Well, now, that's up to the board, Francey,' he said. 'Naturally you will have to take *your* place there now. We'll be able to vote for one another,' he tacked on suavely.

She flushed. 'It's no joke, Bryn.' She waited

until he had resumed his seat and did not tower over her. 'It would be a further whiplash in Carina's face not to offer her a place. I don't know if it will ever sink in that Grandfather chose *me* over her.'

Bryn groaned. 'That's an easy one to answer. You're one hell of a lot brighter than Carina. She was never academically minded. She had no use for further education. She preferred the Grand Tour— swanning around Europe. No, Francey. Carina's beauty might dazzle, but not her brain power.'

'Her beauty dazzles *you*.'

'It *did*. I've admitted that. But only for a while. I don't deny I've made my mistakes, Francey, but I managed not to get *too* carried away. I hate to say it, but there's something a bit off about Carina. The twists in her personality have notched up a few gears since we were together. You saw what she was like today.'

'She had every reason to be shocked,' Francesca said, programmed to be loyal. 'A massive disappointment was at the bottom of her grievances.' Despite the way Carina had acted, Francesca was still moved to defend her cousin. 'She felt betrayed—not only for herself, but for her father.'

'Oh, come off it, Francey.' Bryn spoke impatiently. 'Carina has a total disregard for others. She uses people. It's an inherited trait. You heard the way she went for her father—and in front of the rest of the family. He didn't deserve that, even if he has to take some responsibility for turning her into what she has become. Had *you* been her handsome, clever, *male* cousin, instead of another woman, she would have taken it a whole lot better. Don't you see the last thing Carina wants is to be burdened with heavy responsibilities? She wants to be perfectly free to enjoy herself, to live a life of endless self-indulgence. Frank knew that. Her father knows that. It's the way she was reared, after all. What you have to grasp is this: it's all about *you*. And *her*. Had it been up to Carina, she would have stripped you of your last penny.'

'And would that have been such a great disaster?' Francesca asked ironically. 'I don't want any of this. I can make my own way—and I am.'

Bryn came to sit again, not in the splendid walnut chair but close beside her, bringing with him his immense sexual aura. Oh, this man! What influence he had over her. And there didn't seem to be a thing she could do to lessen its effect. Rather, it was expanding with every passing moment.

'Listen, Francey,' he said, leaning close, so the fine cotton of his shirt brushed against the skin of her arm. 'I know you're a very private person. You like to live out of the limelight. And you've succeeded to an extent. But you're no more entitled to a normal life than I am. That's one of the burdens of being who we are. Privacy goes out the door. Carina revels in attention. She's fortunate in that way. She adores being chased by the paparazzi and being endlessly photographed. That's *her* life. It gives her enormous satisfaction, even if she does like to lodge the odd complaint. You're not like that. But you'll have to concentrate on the main game. You are now in a position to do a great deal for others. There's your saviour.

'There's so much the Foundation can do. Grants to medical science can play a much bigger part than they have in the past. Finding cures for killer diseases, saving lives. It all takes a colossal amount of money. There are so many projects that should have been taken up that the Foundation ignored. It came to the point where the Foundation was simply throwing money at organisations that should have been way down the list. You can change all that. Look what you've already achieved in the area of indigenous art. What about a museum, solely to house aboriginal art, bark paintings and other art forms? You could consider that down the track. Make it self-supporting through a series of initiatives. There are many programmes, crying out for funding. You know my own family's main interest is centred on saving children. You've been to the big charity dinners my grandmother regularly holds. She has carried on my grandfather's work.'

'And she's worshipped,' Francesca said, knowing that for a fact. 'I don't know that I can ever become another Lady Macallan.'

He leaned a little further towards her, surprising her by kissing her cheek. Just an affectionate gesture—one of countless she had received from him over the long years—yet it was more meaningful than the most ardent kiss any other man had ever given her.

'All it's going to take is a little time and experience. You've got everything else. And you've got my support. Any future ideas you might have that you want to discuss or thrash out you'll have my attention.'

'Thank you. I'm really going to need you.' She felt as if she had been launched upon a big, cold and demanding world where power was everything. And now it had been handed to her, an unwilling and unprepared recipient.

'We're going to need one another.' Bryn frowned at some passing thought.

'What if Carina wants to contest the will, as she threatened?' Francesca asked. 'Wouldn't she be justified? She *is* senior to me, and she's Uncle Charles's only child. Besides, she has always known how to get her father on side. The rest of the family will support her.'

Bryn gave a short laugh. 'No, they won't.'

'You sound so sure?' She turned her attention to examining his dynamic face. If only she could peel away all pretence, all the complex layers that lay between them.

'The rest of the family are cool-headed,' Bryn explained briskly. 'Whereas Carina is a hothead. None of them actually trust her. I don't even think they like her. They all know Charles is not right for the job. We've all known it for years. My grandfather spent a great deal of his time priming me. Ultimately for control. I won't deny it. Francis Forsyth didn't make Titan everything it is. My grandfather was the prime mover. Frank became something of an enforcer. Anyway, I knew what my grandfather wanted. *I* want it. Charles doesn't.

Carina can't pretend she has the necessary qualifi-
cations—'

'That's why Grandfather wanted her to marry
you,' Francesca broke in. 'The subject can't be
avoided, Bryn. He planned it all. A marriage
between you and Carrie would have united the
two families. Ended the war. Carina would have
been happy, and well suited to playing the role of
beautiful high society wife.'

'It was a scheme thought up without considering me or my wishes,' Bryn told her with
heavy bluntness.

'What *are* your wishes?' She was terribly
confused. Carina had taken every opportunity to
let her know Bryn belonged to her. And there was
no getting away from the fact she and Bryn had
sustained an intimate relationship, even if Bryn
claimed it was over.

'Maybe *you* would suit me a whole lot better.
What if I wanted to marry *you?*' he asked,
sounding as if he might be serious. 'Let's face it.
You're a very classy lady. Super-smart.' His eyes
were brilliant with mockery, flattery—what? Was
it possible that Bryn, the quintessential business-
man, had simply vaulted to the best possible
option now that *she* was the Forsyth heiress?

Though her heart was racing, it was high time she got herself together. 'I've never for a moment considered it,' she said, amazed she could sound so composed. She had been raised to accept Bryn was for Carina. It was like an alliance, a tradition drawn from the Middle Ages. The knowledge had hung over her head like a sword.

'I think you have, but you've covered it up.' There was real gravity in his voice.

'It's not as if you don't know *why*.' She felt driven to spring up, away from him. It wasn't easy to think when Bryn's power over her was so strong. Those wild moments between them had not only compounded his power a thousandfold, but made it irreversible. It wasn't easy living with a blazing obsession. It was the best and the worst kind of love. From childhood—hadn't she survived because of him?—she had felt so close to him he might have been a kind of twin; a twin she had created lacking a sibling to love. Even as a child she'd had a remarkable insight into Carina's nature. She had always known her cousin didn't love her, never would. She had also known Bryn would forever stand between them.

Bryn, who was desperate to push the issue, had to relent. 'You look played out.' He spoke quietly.

'Why don't I go? You need time on your own. Time to recover and absorb everything that has happened. It's been one long and gut-wrenching day. Death has its own contagion. I know you ached for your grandfather's love and didn't get it, but he must have loved you, Francey, in his own strange way. Take comfort from that. Perhaps he felt enormous guilt about his estrangement from your father? Especially in the light of what happened. Perhaps he thought you were judging him in some way? You were such a serious, *thinking* child, and you had a way of turning those beautiful light-filled eyes on one.'

She was taken aback. Hadn't Carrie said much the same thing? 'Did I? In what way?'

He gave her a faintly twisted smile. 'Oh, you always looked as though you were trying to read one's soul. Maybe Frank found that difficult to face. There were dark places in his soul he wouldn't have wanted you to see. Anyway, Douglas confirmed he was proud of you. That should mean something. He loved Carrie, but he even asked me from time to time why she wasn't getting out there and doing something. He would have liked Carrie to carve out some sort of a career—even getting into the world of fashion, opening boutiques or whatever. She lived for clothes. Neither of us has ever seen her in the same outfit twice.'

'You're not saying he was disappointed in her?' Francesca asked, trying to piece all this together. She'd had no idea.

Bryn shook his head. 'That's a difficult one to answer. It's hard, when you're possessed of a manic energy like Sir Frank was, to view point-less pursuits with a totally tolerant eye. I think he was always going to leave you Daramba.' Abruptly he changed the subject, his dark eyes steadily on her. 'Apart from anything else, he knew how much you loved it.'

'*He* didn't love it,' Francesca said, a catch in her voice. 'He wouldn't go there.'

'Perhaps he had a reason.' Bryn's answer sounded grim. 'He wasn't liked, either as the big boss or a man.' The tribal people had regarded Francis Forsyth as a trespasser on sacred ground. And perhaps a lot *more*. 'How do you feel about his leaving me a half-share?' He captured her gaze. 'I want you to tell me the truth. I can stand it.'

She gave a laugh that held the faintest sob. 'I want *you* more than anyone by my side, Bryn. You already know that. We both love Daramba.'

'That apart,' he said, brushing their mutual love for the great Outback station aside, 'what about my taking control of the business side of the entire operation?'

'You're welcome,' she said wryly.

'I'm going to want to make a lot of changes,' he said, trying to prepare her, reaching for his jacket, then shouldering into it.

How handsome he was. How masculine. She loved the breadth of his shoulders that made his clothes sit so well; the sharp taper that emphasised his lean, narrow waist and hips, and his long, athletic legs. 'Go for it,' she said, trying for lightness on this bleakest of days. 'I have a few ideas of my own you might be interested to hear.'

His brows knotted. 'Of course. I have no intention of going ahead with anything without discussion. We're partners, Francey.'

She nodded, taking enormous comfort from that. 'Partners. I do have a good business head.'

'I know.' He moved towards her with the easy male grace that so characterised him. 'Clever girl! You'll have countless opportunities to bring your expertise to bear.'

'That's if I accept my inheritance,' she replied, her expression grave. 'I want time to think about it. My life would revolve around the Foundation. What time would there be for *me?* I'm serious about my art. I'm serious about helping other artists.' She paused, feeling a jolt of non-acceptance she had to stifle. 'But I fully expect to take my seat on the board of Titan.'

There was a glitter of admiration in his brilliant eyes. 'Sounds like you've already made up your mind.'

She stood there looking at him, in such an agony of need it made her press her hands to her sides. 'It's important for me to know how *you* think and feel.'

'But you *do* know, Francey.' He could read the huge uncertainties that were in her. It was so easy to understand. What she had been offered was almost too big to grasp. 'As far as I'm concerned, you have the brains, the guts and the nerve to carry this off. Do it for everyone's sake. You have the power to change lives for the good. I understand your fears and doubts. But don't get bogged down, thinking your grandfather's will was unfair to Charles and Carina. They've been very handsomely provided for. Your grandfather knew what he was doing.'

For once let Forsyth and Macallan be on the

same side, he prayed. Only with Francesca at the helm was that possible. 'Now, I'm off,' he said briskly, before his control snapped and he pulled her into his arms. God knows he wanted to, but he knew what would happen next. Carina had convinced Francesca of her lies, and her bullying had made it nearly impossible for Francesca to accept that someone might want her instead of her cousin. Whatever she *said,* whatever barriers she threw up, he knew she was very vulnerable to him. His role, however, was to shield and protect her.

At his imminent departure Francesca knew a moment of pure panic. 'I don't want you to go.' Her need for him rose to overwhelm her.

'Yes, you do,' he said. 'I don't want you weighed down with emotion, Francey. Some things have to stay on hold.'

That sobered her. She made a huge effort to pull herself together, walking with him to the door. 'So much to do, Bryn,' she said, determined not to crumble under the weight of it all. 'So many meetings. So many people to get to know. So much information I'll have to read and try to absorb.'

'One day at a time, Francey,' he advised, moving

further away. Her aura was more intense than he had ever known. 'Don't let it crowd you. All you have to do is remember you're not alone.' He didn't bend to kiss her cheek. He wasn't *that* much of a knight in shining armour. 'What do you say we fly out to Daramba the weekend after next?' he asked. 'Both of us will definitely be needing a break by then.'

Her face lit up from within, its illumination filling him with surging desire. 'That sounds wonderful!'

Resolutely he opened the door, keeping his hand fixed firmly to the handsome brass knob. 'Good. I'll arrange it. You can bring a chaperon if you want,' he added, only half in jest. 'Ring you tomorrow. I'm off now to see my girls.'

She knew he was referring to Lady Macallan and his mother, Annette, who shared the beautiful historic Macallan mansion. It was a far cry from the Forsyth mausoleum. After the tragic death of her husband, Annette Macallan had suffered a long period of depression that had ended in a breakdown. Sir Theo and Lady Macallan had looked after her like a beloved daughter.

'Give them my love,' she said. 'Tell them I'll speak to them soon. I need to speak to Elizabeth as well. Grandfather didn't find it in his heart to leave her even a small memento.'

'What heart?' Bryn asked with a brief, discordant laugh. If Francis Forsyth had thought he would win the Macallans over by leaving him a half-share in the Forsyth pastoral empire he had thought wrong. Frank Forsyth's treachery had been like a knife in the back to his grandfather. Sir Theo had died knowing what a deadly serpent he'd had for a lifelong friend.

The days that followed gave Francesca her first real understanding of the power and far-reaching influence of great wealth. There was an endless list of concerns she had to address, and then, when she had given them her full attention, endeavour to prioritise.

She had a model to go on. The Macallan Foundation, among other things, funded medical research into childhood diseases. That was their main focus. The Macallan Foundation built research centres and hospitals, and awarded endowments and scholarships to educate doctors not only for the home front but for third world countries as well. The Macallan name was enormously respected. She wanted the same respect for the

Forsyth Foundation. She wanted to be assured that the Forsyth Foundation would be doing the work it was meant to do, much in the way of the Macallan Foundation—which Bryn administered.

If she needed advice—and she desperately did—he was the best person to turn to. Lord knew he was approachable enough, for all the burden of responsibilities placed upon him. But even knowing this Francesca felt she had to spare him and bring her own perfectly good mind to bear on it all. She refused to be the figurehead her grandfather had been. She had to start building a new life for herself. Not one she had wanted, but one she realised offered her the greatest opportunity for doing good. She had to start learning from everyone who was in a position to help her. When she was ready she was going to make changes—she had all but decided already on a glaring few—but for now she needed a tremendous amount of help.

The paperwork alone was staggering. Her routine had entirely changed as her life had speeded up dramatically. She woke at five instead of seven. Leapt out of bed. She went to bed very late. Yet even with that timetable she felt *energised*. There was so much to be done. A big plus was that she met daily with people who were not only in a position to help her, but were going out of their way to do so, seemingly delighted to be called on. That gave her a great confidence boost. Bryn left messages for her constantly, to tell her to get in touch with this one or that. All whiz kids who could run things for her as she wanted and then report back. She had to learn early how to delegate or go under, he told her, speaking from experience and the benefit of his own heavy workload.

She needed secretaries—all kinds of secretaries. Even press secretaries to front for her. She had endured a very scary onslaught of attention from the media almost from the minute the news of her elevation within the Forsyth family had broken. She needed people around her she could trust. *Really* trust. Loyalty was top of her agenda. Valerie Scott, a senior foundation secretary, was working for her now.

Valerie was a very attractive, highly competent divorcee in her late forties, tall and svelte, with snapping dark eyes and improbably rich dark red hair. She dressed well, with discreet good jewellery and accessories. As a Hartford—her maiden name—she was a member of an old Establishment family that had not only fallen on bad times but

gone bust. A string of dodgy investments had
figured somewhere along the way, Francesca
seemed to recall. After Valerie's marriage break-
up from a successful stockbroker, who had left her
for a look-alike twenty years younger, Sir Francis
had given Valerie a job. Her 'office' was an open
area right outside his door, with Valerie seated
behind an antique desk of very fine rosewood with
more of the ormolu, lions' masks and feet her
grandfather had favoured.

It wouldn't have surprised Francesca in the least
to learn that Valerie had become more than a secretary to her grandfather. He'd had countless affairs,
yet still been a man incapable of true love. Still,
Francesca found her new secretary courteous and
obliging, with an air of having everything fully
under control. Time would tell. At the moment
Valerie was proving extremely useful. She had no
mind to replace her. She certainly didn't want to put
any woman out of a well-paid job—especially one
who had to fend for herself. For the time being things
could continue as they were. She didn't want to
become a suspicious person—it wasn't her nature—
but sadly she had entered a very suspicious world.

Bryn had taken time out to fully alert her to
security threats. The offices and executive confer-

ence room were regularly swept for bugs. Telephones, cellular and cordless, were by their very nature a threat. If royalty could have their phones tapped, so could anyone. Some years back a small transmitter had been discovered to be concealed inside her Uncle Charles's phone. She knew her grandfather from that day on had upgraded security measures, making sure all telephones and audio visual equipment were removed from conference rooms where confidential matters were discussed. Even so, more and more sophisticated devices were coming on to the market. Trusting one's staff was extremely important. A strip search apart, who knew what anyone was hiding? Thank God it hadn't come to that.

It would have given Francesca the greatest pleasure and satisfaction to have been able to take Carina on board. A different Carina, who herself was open to change. But Carina continued to complain bitterly to anyone who would listen about how she and her father had been robbed. Court action, however, to overturn their grandfather's will did not eventuate. The view of the public was that the *right* heiress had been handed the job. The public was rarely wrong.

'Leopards don't change their spots,' Bryn remarked during a late-night telephone conversation. They both had such a packed agenda it was difficult to meet. 'You can't seriously believe Carina would involve herself in *any* kind of work?'

'It could make her feel better about herself. It could be the start of some sort of reconciliation between us.' Francesca spoke hopefully. 'I don't want this feud to continue, Bryn.'

'Dream on, Santa Francesca!' A theatrical groan travelled down the wires. 'Carina doesn't share your concern for the less fortunate. She thinks by looking gorgeous she's more than repaying her debt to society.'

Gradually Francesca was brought around to thinking she might ask Elizabeth to come on board. She still wanted people she could *trust*. If needs be, with her life. She no longer felt as safe as she once had. She was a sitting duck in so many ways. She had her allies, but she had to become a hard-headed realist. She had her enemies too. People who were lying low, waiting for her to fail. But Elizabeth was different. Elizabeth had raised her. Elizabeth had always been on the charity circuit, but Francesca thought she could do a great deal more if she were allowed to.

She spoke to Bryn about it, over a hastily arranged lunch date.

'An interesting idea—maybe a bit provocative, given the estrangement in the family.' He had taken his time to reply. 'You know that Lady Antonia and I have done everything we possibly could to get my mother involved in our foundation, but her heart doesn't seem to be in anything any more. Not since my father died. My mother is a one-man woman.' His sigh was full of a deep regret. 'But I have to say I understand it.'

'Do you think Annette would help me?' she stunned him by asking.

In the middle of taking a bite out of a bread roll he coughed, then quickly swallowed a mouthful of water. 'God, Francey!' he exclaimed, touching a lean hand to his scratched throat.

'I've shocked you?'

'You have. But shock on.'

She kept her eyes on him. 'Annette and I get on so well together. You know we do.'

He nodded. 'Okay, so you're very sensitive and intuitive. Both my grandmother and my mother have a soft spot for you. And it's *you* more than anyone outside myself that my mother confides in. She knows whatever she says to you you'll be certain to keep it between yourselves. My mother doesn't trust a lot of people. With good reason. But she trusts you.'

Francesca did something she had never dared to do before. His lean tanned hand was lying on the table. She reached across and closed her hand over it, interlocking their fingers. 'That goes both ways,' she assured him, feeling stronger for his touch. 'I trust Annette. I've told her a lot of things I haven't told anyone else.'

'Including me?' Did she know his senses were being heightened to a painful edge? He wanted to pick up her hand and carry it to his mouth. But he knew that would only scare her off.

'Yes, including you.' She blushed, rose mantling her beautiful skin. 'But just think of this for a moment. Lady Macallan is such an exceptional woman that Annette might consider herself unable to act on her level. But with me? She's known me since I was a baby. I'm the merest beginner.'

'Are you really? The merest beginner? You'd have fooled me.' Bryn's brilliant black eyes glittered, but in his way he was already tossing this extraordinary idea around in his head. 'You could ask her.'

'I have your permission?' There was a quick flare of joy in her eyes. 'You don't know how much I appreciate that. We both know people might question why Annette Macallan would choose to join the *Forsyth* Foundation in any capacity.'

'Count on it,' Bryn confirmed bluntly.

'Oddly enough, I think she might enjoy it. As much love as there is between Lady Macallan and Annette, Lady Macallan is a formidable woman— a true personage. It's in *that* sense your mother might feel overshadowed.'

Bryn gave her a fathomless stare. 'She told you that?'

'No, no, no!' Francesca shook her head. 'Your mother would never say such a thing. Lady Macallan is her second mother. She adores her. It's just something I sense. Surely you've sensed it too?'

When he answered his tone was crisp enough to crackle. 'God, Francey, I'm confronted by this every day of my life,' he said. 'I'm very proud of my grandmother. What a woman! And I think I get some of my own strengths from her. But she and I have been waiting for years now for my mother to take back her life. She was only a girl when my father married her. Just nineteen. She had me less than two years later. Dad was her lord and master. He didn't aim to be that. It just happened. They were very much in love, right up until the end. We were all so damned happy. Too happy. One shouldn't ever tempt the gods. After Dad was killed much of my mother died too. Her own parents—my Barrington grandparents—didn't stand by her. Oh, they tried for a while, but gradually they became impatient with her. She was supposed to pull out of it after a certain period of mourning. She didn't. I'm sure she'll be saying my father's name with her last breath.'

'And who's to say he won't be waiting for her?' Francesca spoke gently to this man she loved, wanted to be with through eternity. 'Millions and millions of people believe in a resurrection, an afterlife.'

Bryn's sigh was jagged. 'Be that as it may, we have to get through what life we have *now*. Speak to my mother if you want. Anything that helps her helps me. But don't be disappointed if she gently rejects the idea.'

'That's fine. I won't press her. I understand her pain. I understand the way she felt nearly destroyed without your father. But she did live for you.'

A terrible frustration showed itself in Bryn's eyes. 'She can't continue to live for me, Francey. She has to live for herself. God, she's only just turned fifty. She's a beautiful woman. Yet she has locked herself away for years. Dad would never have wanted that. He loved her so much he would only want her to be happy.'

Francesca smiled in an effort to relieve his tension. 'Let me talk to her. In some ways I'm not in a good situation, am I? A lot of people are waiting for me to screw up. Carina is hoping one of these days I'll simply *disappear* into the desert and never come back. I need help. No one knows that more than you. I want a woman—women, as it happens, as Elizabeth is another—I can trust. I'll put it to Annette that way. I won't be asking a great deal of her. I'll do as you say. Take it day by day.'

Bryn gave a hollow laugh. 'If you can get my mother out of the house I'll worship at your feet for ever.' Though wasn't he already doing just that? 'Did I tell you, you look stunningly beautiful?'

'Yes, you did.' Colour mounted beneath her flawless skin. 'It's a new outfit. I didn't go shopping. No time. I asked Adele Bennett to pick me out a wardrobe, which she did, and then brought it all over.'

'You couldn't have asked for anyone better,' Bryn said, his eyes travelling over her. She wore a sleeveless navy silk dress that showed off the elegant set of her shoulders and her slender arms. The dress was very simple in design but striking in effect, with broad strokes of colour as if she, the artist, had taken to it with a brush: violet, yellow, and a marvellous splash of electric blue that put him in mind of a kingfisher's plumage. It looked wonderful on her. Adele Bennett he had met at various functions. She owned exclusive boutiques in several state capitals. She must have relished the job of outfitting Francesca, with her beauty, her height and her willowy figure.

'You like what you see?' she prompted gently, though she felt more as if she was being consumed by his brilliant black gaze.

'Francey, I have to say *yes*.' He threw up his dark head, then gave a swift glance at his watch. 'Shame we have to part, but there it is. I have a meeting at two-thirty.' He lifted a hand to signal the waiter, who came on the double. 'By the way, I thought we'd take *this* weekend off to visit Daramba.' He spoke as if he wouldn't brook any argument. 'I've cleared my schedule sufficiently to warrant it. I can't and won't wait another week. It's absolutely essential to find time for relaxation. We've both been doing precious little of that.

So see you keep the weekend free. Understood?' He lifted his eyes from the plate where he had placed his platinum credit card and smiled.

Such a smile! His whole face caught light.

'Understood,' she said calmly, when inside she felt wildly happy. She had held the thought of them being together at Daramba all these long days. The thought had sustained her—a wonderful weekend that was waiting for her. And she had no intention of taking along a chaperon. A chaperon was all very well for the old Francesca Forsyth. But the old Francesca had been forced out of her shell. She was now the Forsyth heiress, like it or not. She no longer lived her old life. She no longer lived like a normal person. She even felt emboldened enough to throw her own cap in the ring. Maybe Bryn had been right all along. He *was* a free man.

It was getting on towards four on the Friday afternoon prior to their trip to Daramba when Carina of all people burst through the door, bringing with her a whoosh of perfumed air.

'Carina!' Francesca rose from her desk, aware that Valerie Scott was hovering in the background, wringing her hands and looking extremely agitated. Obviously she had taken fright. 'It's all right, Valerie,' she said, a model of calm.

It was doubtful if anyone on the planet would be capable of stopping a Carina hell-bent on gaining entry to what after all was their late grandfather's resplendent office. Francesca had reduced the splendour considerably by stripping it of its more florid touches and personalising the space. She had taken down two of the blue chip colonial paintings that would fetch a small fortune and replaced them with one of her best paintings, which she had held back from sale, an Outback landscape, and one of Nellie Napirri's stunningly beautiful waterlily paintings. In a very short time they had proved to be excellent conversation starters, putting visitors at their ease.

'Yes, go back to work,' Carina instructed the woman in imperious tones. 'And never try to stop me from entering this office again.'

Scarlet in the face and mottled in the throat, Valerie made a valiant effort to defend herself. 'I wasn't trying to *stop* you, Ms Forsyth. I was merely trying to let Ms Forsyth know you were here.'

'It didn't look like that to me,' Carina said in her clipped, high-handed voice. 'You can shut the door.'

'Of course.' A deeply mortified Valerie was already attempting to do that very thing.

Inwardly churning—the cheek of her!—
Francesca waved her cousin into a leather chair
opposite. One of their grandfather's choices, it
should swallow her up. 'Is there something you
want, Carrie?'

Carina remained standing. 'What do you think
I want?' she challenged, already falling into what
could be a question-for-question session.

'I have no idea. Why don't you tell me?'
Francesca invited, surprised her tone was so easy
and natural, and giving a thought to her composed
inner strength—which was growing by the day. As
ever, Carina looked a million dollars. A goddess
of glamour in a white linen suit cinched tightly at
the waist by a wide gold metallic belt. There were
strappy gold stilettos on her feet, and a very luxu-
rious white and gold leather tote bag over her
shoulder. No wonder she had tempted Bryn.
Carina would make the blood run hot in an
Eskimo's veins.

Carina frowned, carelessly plonking her very ex-
pensive bag on the carpeted floor before dipping
into the plush seat, showing off almost the entire
length of her very good legs. No neat ankle crosses
for Carina. Her wonderful hair had been cut to clear
the shoulder, side parted, full of natural volume.

'How are you, by the way?' She looked up to fix Francesca with a piercing blue gaze growing more and more like their grandfather's.

'I'm fine, thank you. And you?' What was this all about? Francesca thought. Was Carina's bad-girl side in remission? Dared she hope? The word *epiphany* sprung to mind. Maybe Carina had had one on the way over.

Carina flicked a frowning, all-encompassing glance around the vast room—the wall-to-wall bookcases crammed with weighty tomes, a magnificent pair of terrestrial and celestial globes on mahogany stands, the large paintings, memorabilia, dozens of silver-framed photographs of Sir Francis with famous people, trophies and awards—then said sarcastically, 'Made changes, I see. Like to show off you're such a clever chick.' Her eyes moved to the painting of the waterlily lagoon surrounded by aquatic plants. 'I don't like *that!* Too highly coloured. Aboriginal work, isn't it?'

'Nellie Napirri,' Francesca said. 'I love it. The colours are very true to our lily-filled billabongs. Surely you recognise that? You've seen enough of them. It's not a misty Monet, though I'm absolutely certain Monet would have loved it too. You mightn't be aware of it, Carrie, but Nellie's work is fetching big money these days.'

Carina made a face that signified complete un-interest. 'She'll only blow it on the rest of her tribe. That's the way they are. The place looks okay—more feminine, I guess—but you scarcely fit into Gramps's shoes.'

'Neither of us do, come to think of it,' Francesca answered evenly.

'Are you happy?' Carina shot at her.

Francesca pushed the file she had been reading to one side. 'Off hand, I'd give it an eight out of ten. But I've been much too busy to question my state of mind, Carina. Would you like to tell me what you're here for? Not that I'm not pleased to see you. I *am*. I don't want bad feeling between us. You're my cousin. We're family.'

'Some family, right?' For a moment Carina regarded the impressive array of gold gem-studded bracelets on her right arm—emerald, ruby, amethyst, topaz, a couple more. On her left she wore a solid gold watch set with diamonds; a diamond-set gold hoop encircled the narrow wrist above it. Every mugger in the world would have thought her a dream target. 'Look, I'll come straight to the point. It's not easy for me, but I want to apologise for the way I've been acting. I've been a damned fool. It's just…'

'You were shocked.' Francesca hastened to help her cousin out, even though she knew she might never rate another apology in her life. 'You've been led to believe everything would be different. I felt the same way.'

'Ah, well…' Carina sighed, a recent convert to being philosophical. 'I think Gramps was way ahead of Dad and me.' She gave Francesca a wry smile. 'Dad is a lot happier these days. Bless him. Had Gramps left him in control he would surely have died of a heart attack before his time. As for me! Want the truth?'

'Yes, please.' Lord knew she didn't want more lies.

'Doing what I do makes me happy,' Carina confessed, as though Francesca had never for a moment known. 'I wouldn't want to be cooped up like you, trying to get your head around mind-boggling stuff. I know you're smart, but Gramps left too heavy a burden on those bony shoulders. You're too thin, you know that? Men don't like skin and bone. Anyway, very few people ever take women seriously in business. I expect you've already found that out?'

'I could name you any number of women being taken very seriously in business, Carrie,' she said. 'Maybe you're not as much in touch with the current scene as you thought. People have been very helpful, as a matter of fact. I have a great deal to learn, but I seem to be coping. I don't do things on my own. As I said, I have help.'

'Of course! The staff would probably be able to run the place without you,' Carina flashed back, a teeny crack showing in the *bonhomie*. 'First thing you want to do is get rid of the thumper outside the door.'

Francesca struggled with that for a moment. 'Thumper?' Her black eyebrows rose. 'I thought a thumper was a nightclub bouncer?' Carina, big on the nightclub scene, would know.

'Whatever!' Carina threw her head back so forcefully her hair bounced. 'I don't like her. She was having an affair with Gramps—did you know?'

'Well, I'm sure *Gramps* put the hard word on her.' Francesca spoke very dryly, to her own amazement. She had never called her grandfather Gramps in her entire life. 'Grandfather wasn't everything he should have been.'

'Oh, hold on!' Carina was about to take umbrage

on their grandfather's behalf—took a short pause for reflection and thought better of it. 'Why *her?*'

'Being right outside the door might have helped, don't you think? But I've never much liked gossip, Carrie. Valerie is divorced. Grandfather was a widower—'

'With one helluva sex life!' Carina gave one of her little whoops. 'If there was a Nobel Prize awarded for a lifetime of having lovers it would have been given to Gramps. I suppose that's what did him in at the end. Thought he was God's gift to women, isn't that right? Maybe he had a premonition he was going to die. There *was* another will, you know.'

Francesca nodded. 'Yes, Douglas told me.'

'Still retaining that old fool?' Carina reacted with disgust.

Francesca remained calm and confident. Just a taste of power had given her a massive injection of those much needed qualities. 'I trust him, Carrie. He has a fine reputation. And he's gentlemanly.'

Carina's mouth down turned sceptically. 'At least that's what he likes to present to the world. I bet he can talk dirty just like the rest of us.'

'Now, that, Carrie, defies belief. I must lead a different life to you, as well. I've never talked dirty in my life.'

'No, you're a terminal Miss Goody Two-Shoes,' Carina said with affectionate contempt. 'You really ought to stop. Or maybe you intend to? Bryn tells me you're off to Daramba for the weekend?' Her tone made it clear she thought Francesca knew she and Bryn were back in touch and didn't give a hoot.

It took a tremendous effort for Francesca to keep the shock off her face. 'I didn't realise you were speaking to him these days?' She told herself Carina was a pathological liar. But that posed the question: who else knew? She hadn't said a word to anyone. She couldn't believe Bryn went about advertising his intentions. He operated on the basis that one could never be too careful. Then there was the fact he had never mentioned having contact with Carina, let alone a reconciliation.

'Oh, come off it, sweetie,' Carina mocked, as though she knew every thought that was running riot through Francesca's head. 'We've both known Bryn since we were kids. Do you honestly think Bryn and I would remain out of touch for long?' she jeered. 'Actually, it was Bryn who made the first move. Surely he told you? Maybe not. My intuition says he didn't. He plays his cards close to his chest. But that's half the reason I'm here. It was Bryn who suggested it. He really does think everything through. He says it's not wise for any of us to continue this feud in public or in private. Besides, the last people I want to quarrel with are you and Bryn. How can I put this?' Her stunning face took on an unfamiliar expression of earnestness, even soul-searching. 'I *need* you both. The people all around me I can't trust. I don't for one moment think they're for real. They're all over me to my face; treacherous behind my back. Envy, of course. You were never like that, Francey. Neither was Bryn. We're all just too bloody rich for most people. They hate it. Money has to stick with money. It's Them versus *Us!*'

'Sounds a bit like paranoia to me, Carrie,' Francesca said. 'Besides, we *do* get all the perks. I can't afford to see it your way. I'm now dealing with so many people from all walks of life. So, when did Bryn tell you we were off to Daramba?' She spoke as if it were of no great importance when inwardly she was feeling sick and vulnerable. It had only been over lunch on Wednesday that Bryn had suggested bringing forward their trip.

'Yesterday, I think,' Carina said, rolling her eyes upwards, as though yesterday's date was written on the ceiling. 'Yes, it had to be yesterday. I'd go with you, but Daramba has never held the same fascination for me as it has for you and Bryn. The break should do you good. I'm off to Sydney tomorrow myself. The Cartwrights are having another one of their gala parties. All the glitterati will be there. I have the most incredible dress! You'd love it! Not that you could pull it off. It's so darn sexy. Softly, softly does it with you, doesn't it, luvvy? I, on the other hand, like to shake people up.'

'No one better at it in the country,' Francesca assured her. 'Have you spoken to your mother?' She tacked that on as though it were an afterthought. In reality she was trying to divine whether her cousin was on the level. People expressed themselves in so many ways. Speech, of course, but also body language—the way they moved, their hands, eyes. Wasn't there a theory that the eyes moved left or right according to whether one was telling the truth or not? The trouble was she couldn't remember which side indicated the lie.

'Next one on my list,' Carina told her with a saddened little smile. 'It's taken me over-long to rebuild my bridges. What say we do lunch early next week? I think it would be good for the press to see us out and about together.'

'Next week is all pencilled in, I'm afraid, Carrie,' Francesca said. It was true enough. 'Maybe the following week?'

'I'll have to think. Let that secretary do some of your work,' Carina suggested crossly. 'It won't hurt her. What's her name again?'

'Valerie Scott. Surely you've met her any number of times before? You were always calling in on Grandfather.'

'Unlike you,' Carina abruptly fired up, fixing Francesca with a steely eye. 'I've met her, of course, but some people you just meet and forget. It's people like me that make a lifelong impact. That hair has to go, and she could lose some weight. No wonder she lost hubby. Did you see the size of her backside?'

'You're too figure-conscious, Carrie,' Francesca sighed. 'Valerie is a very attractive woman.'

'One can never be too figure-conscious.' Carina shuddered, retrieving her tote. 'I hate that matronly upholstered look. I'm almost tempted to tell her.'

'Please don't,' Francesca begged as Carina rose to her feet. 'Sure I can't offer you a cup of coffee?'

'No time!' Carina gave a clatter of her heavily weighted down arm. 'I'm having dinner tonight with someone you know.'

'Oh, who's that?' Francesca looked up casually, but her hands were gripping the edge of her desk hard, the knuckles showing white. If Carina said Bryn, their trip would be off.

'Greg Norbett.'

Francesca's fingers unlocked as the ferocious tension disappeared. 'Greg? Isn't he still married?' she asked, as calmly as she could. 'Gosh, it's only been a couple of years.' They had both attended Greg's wedding to a lovely girl.

'It's at the separation stage.' Carina spoke carelessly, as though it were only a hop, step and a jump to divorce. 'You need to be married at least a year before you get a divorce. Otherwise it's just tacky. What was it he saw in *you?*' she joshed, her blue eyes full of cousinly teasing.

'Why don't you ask him?' Francesca said. Greg Norbett had actually proposed to her after a fundraising party. A surprise because she'd never encouraged a relationship with him. What a good thing she hadn't been attempted to accept Greg's proposal, given his limited attention span. She felt very sad about his wife. It wasn't very sporting,

Carina sleeping with other women's husbands. In some respects Carina rated a moral zero.

Francesca came around her desk to accompany her cousin to the door, though it was more like a flat-out sprint, keeping up with Carina's pace.

'Have a great weekend, Francey!' Carina turned to say. 'I *mean* that!' She bent slightly—she was tall, especially in those stiletto heels—to give Francesca an air peck. 'Bryn likes to look out for you. He's been at it for most of your life.' It was said in a tone that in someone else would have been gentle amusement, but somehow from Carina sounded snide. 'Can I give you a word of advice?' She swept on before Francesca could say yay or nay. 'I'm much more savvy in the ways of the world than you are.'

'No argument there,' Francesca said.

'Enjoy yourself,' Carina told her magnanimously. 'But whatever you do, *don't trust Bryn.* He's a master manipulator.'

'I suppose we all are from time to time.'

Carina's brows rose. 'Be that as it may, Francesca, I trusted Bryn Macallan to my cost. He was the love of my life. He took my virginity.'

It *was* possible, but the new Francesca wasn't sure she believed her. 'Sure you hadn't abandoned it before that?'

Carina levelled her with an affronted frown. 'Have your little joke. I expected you to fly to Bryn's defence, but you know yourself, Francey, I'm a far better judge of character than you are. I know Bryn's a sizzlingly exciting man. Zillions of women can only get to dream about a guy like Bryn, but *I* had him for the longest possible time. *I* was the one to clock up the hours. And where did it get me? Absolutely nowhere. No engagement, no wedding, like I'd been promised. Worst of all, no damned respect. D'you know what I think?'

'Please tell me.' Francesca remained outwardly calm.

'He has turned his attention to *you*.' Carina whipped that out like a master stroke. 'Bryn doesn't need me any more. He doesn't need any more money. It's power he's after. That's what he's all about. That's what he *does*. Just like Gramps. We women are only pawns. It has never been any different, right down the centuries. We get *used*. I certainly was, and I don't want it to happen to you. I really do care about you, Francey. This is *family* now. You know what they say?'

'Blood's thicker than water?' Francesca hazarded a guess. She already knew that wasn't always the case. 'So, what do you suggest I do?'

'Don't *ever* let him into your bed,' Carina warned her, regarding Francesca like a Mother Superior with a wavering novice. 'He'll try it, but don't worry. Just make sure it doesn't happen. He'll be everything you ever wanted or wished for, but there will be a price to pay. He'll have you, body and soul. God knows, I've had to fight hard to free myself of the madness.'

Francesca knew she wasn't exaggerating. 'Has the madness gone?' she asked gently. Tender at heart, she was profoundly sorry for her pain. Carina was her cousin, after all. They had spent much of their lives together.

Carina backed up to the door, looking disturbingly near tears, which further upset Francesca. Carina never cried. Not even at their grandfather's funeral, when one would have thought she could have squeezed out a few. 'It gets less and less every day,' she said, blinking her eyes valiantly. 'There are plenty of other distractions. Like poor Greg. He's such a bore! His poor little wife should sue him for causing her grievous mental distress. I'm twenty-six going on twenty-seven, Francey, and I've relinquished all faith in men.' The genuine unhappiness in Carina's brilliant blue eyes said more than a thousand words ever could.

'Oh, Carrie, I'm sorry.' Francesca reached out to take gentle hold of her cousin's arm. Love was the very devil! This had to be terrible for the proud Carina. 'Twenty-six is no age. You're so beautiful, so much admired. You have the world at your feet. There are plenty of good men out there.'

Carina gave a laugh to cover her distress. 'Not the ones I've encountered. As long as I can save *you*. That's all I care about. Don't take a gamble on Bryn, Francey. You'll *never* win.' She opened the heavy door, then stepped into the wide carpeted corridor, totally ignoring Valerie Scott, who sat at her desk, head bowed so close to her work she had to be going cross-eyed. 'I'll be in touch,' she promised with a big smile. 'Next time you take off I might come with you. Out there we can really bond.'

Francesca said nothing. Bonding wasn't an activity Carina had paid much attention to in the past. But there was always hope. Wasn't hope supposed to spring eternal? Could a leopard change its spots? The answer in nature was a resounding *no!* Applied to humans, the verdict wasn't so reliable. What *exactly* had Carina come to tell her? Was this another one of her strategies? Changed spots or not, she didn't fancy the idea of putting her head in a leopard's mouth.

After Carina had gone on her way, leaving a minefield of possibilities, Francesca withdrew to her office, closing the door. It wasn't her practice to do it all the time, but she did it now, directing a little sympathetic smile Valerie's way. Poor Valerie! Carina had been very rough on her. Then again, there was the possibility Carina was in the early stages of turning herself around. Who could deny there were great life-changing forces constantly at work?

One good thing about being the official Forsyth heiress. If she disappeared, even in the Outback, people would notice.

CHAPTER FIVE

THEY flew into Daramba well before noon. Once over the vast station Bryn brought the King Air down low, so they could get a closer look at the condition of the land. The endless miles of wild-flowers had all but vanished, ready to reappear with the next Wet Season's good rains, but the ancient landscape—the infinite Inland Sea of pre-history—still frothed in blossom from the trees. Daramba was in prime condition, the fiery red earth thickly sown with thick Mitchell and Flinders grass, the ubiquitous spinifex, salt bush, hop bush and the succulent pink *parakeelya* cattle liked to feed on. There were clusters of billabongs, three or four linked, before a break of a few miles streaked away to the horizon, the iridescent blue of the sky holding a couple of white clouds, like giant cotton wool balls. No rain in them. No rain anywhere over a state more than twice the size of Texas.

The great system of water channels that ran like

intricate lacework all over the Channel Country glittered in the sun, some silver, others dark green, with occasionally a cloudy opal-blue or lime-green, framed by the dark green fringing trees that grew along the sandy banks. It created a whole kaleidoscope of colour. And there was movement as well as colour. A mob of brumbies with a long-tailed bay at the front—tall and powerful for a wild horse—its harem behind, the half-grown foals alongside, suddenly shot into view from a thick screen of bauhinias, probably taking fright at the sound of the plane's engines. They were a marvellous sight in flight, and because of easy access to feed and water in glossy condition.

Stockmen on the ground looked up and waved their dusty hats as they made their passes over campsites and holding yards where fat cattle were penned almost bumper to bumper. In the middle distance a big mob was moving like the giant Rainbow Snake of aboriginal legend, twisting and turning as they made their way to one of the billabongs with a couple of stockmen riding back and forth among them, urging the beasts on and keeping them in an orderly forma-tion. They didn't look as if they needed much urging, Francesca thought.

Away on the western border of the station, the midday heat was reflected off the ramparts of the Hill Country, with its turrets, minarets and crenellations, its secret caves with their well-guarded aboriginal rock paintings. At this time of day the eroded hills with their fantastic shapes glowed furnace-red. Early morning they were a soft light pink that deepened during the morning to rose, and then the fiery red of high noon. Late afternoon they changed to a haunting deep purple, incredible against the flaming backdrop of the sunset, then, as the sun dropped towards the horizon, faded to a misty lilac. Night fell abruptly in the Outback, like a vast black velvet curtain decorated with a billion desert stars. Now, in the noon fire, the whole area was bathed in the shimmery veil of mirage.

Francesca felt so thrilled to be back she was a little shaky with it. She knew she had to relax, but her whole body was zinging. Two days alone with Bryn! What ecstasy! She hadn't told him Carina had called in to the office to see her. By the same token, she hadn't questioned him in any way regarding Carina, much less mentioned how it had hurt her—hurt like the very devil—to hear he had told Carina about their planned weekend on the station they now jointly owned and that they were back in contact. She wasn't looking for conflict. In a way she was considering opting out of the whole business of Bryn, Carina and herself. The infamous love triangle. Carina wasn't cured any more than she was. They were both hopelessly in love with Bryn. But she wanted more than anything to cherish this time they would have together. Life being what it was, it might be all she was going to get.

'Homestead coming up now.' Bryn turned his head towards her. What was he really saying to her with that beautiful heart-wrenching smile?

She smiled back. She was a woman in love. She didn't even care if she wasn't disguising the fact all that well. Most probably she was giving herself away with the flush in her cheeks and the sparkle in her eyes. Every second she had with the man she loved was important. Love, the most powerful of all alchemies, made it very difficult to get and then keep one's bearings.

On the ground he caught her hand, walking her to the waiting station Jeep. Her faint trembling was conveying itself to him like a warm vibration. He had always felt immensely protective of Francesca when she was a child, then right through adolescence, and even now when she was all grown up. A woman.

'You're trembling, Francey. What's the matter?' He looked down at her, knowing he wanted her more than anything else in the world. Knowing too, he had reached the point where he was past pretending. But he had to tread carefully. The last thing he could afford to do was startle her like one could spook a nervous, high-strung filly. So he waited. It would be so much better for her to come to him.

The voice that he found so alluring was full of excitement. 'Nothing's the matter. I feel great. You know how I love this place.'

'Best place in the world!' he confirmed.

'You don't know how much joy it gives me to know we're of the same mind.'

She turned up her face to him so trustingly. It was a poetic face, he thought. Lyrical in style, the contours delicate where Carina's were bold and arresting. His mother always said Francesca reminded her of one of her favourite actresses, who had died in the mid 1960s: Vivien Leigh— Lady Olivier. One of the reasons he had bought the DVD of *Gone With the Wind* had been to see if Francesca was really as much like Vivien Leigh as his mother always claimed. She was. The resemblance lay in the high-arching black brows, the light eyes, the sensitive cut of the mouth, the curling cloud of dark hair, and again that delicate bone structure.

'Why are you staring at me like that?' She gave him a smile that tore at his heart. 'It's really me.'

'It is indeed.' How could a woman project such sensuality and an airy lightness of manner at one and the same time? He moved, rather abruptly, to open the passenger door for her.

Francesca followed, a little puzzled by his reaction. Today he wore a light blue and white checked open-necked shirt and blue jeans, the short sleeves of his shirt exposing the sleek muscles in his darkly tanned upper arms. He was a beautiful man. How many years now was it she had been sketching Bryn? She'd lost count. He was a marvellous subject, and one of her strengths was capturing the essence of her sitter, whether they were aware she was sketching them or not, which was often the case. Bryn actually owned dozens of her sketches; had grabbed them off her. Many he'd had framed in ebony and hung in groups. But he didn't possess a single sketch she had made of him. His mother had many. So did Lady Macallan. Both women had told her they treasured them.

'This *is* Bryn!' Annette always said, with motherly pride in her eyes.

As she went to get in the Jeep, Bryn laid his hand briefly on her shoulder. 'I've got something to tell you.'

At once she drew back, stifling a gasp. *No, no, Bryn! Don't spoil it.*

'It's not *that* bad.' He frowned, taken aback by the play of emotion across her face. Was it distress? What did she think he was going to say? 'I gave Jili and Jacob the weekend off to spend in the Alice,' he quickly explained. 'I think we can survive without them, don't you?'

'You did what?' Surprise filled her voice as enormous relief pumped in.

'You have some objection?'

'I thought we were equal partners?' She was struggling against the compulsion to simply fold herself against him, to surrender to the blazing force that was in him, let it *scorch* her. But she had to be careful. She had to think everything through. Wasn't it a woman's unattainability that made her so desirable? History certainly suggested it.

'We are. I hope we always will be.'

'You mean that?'

'Don't you?' He pinned her gaze, his own fathomless.

'Nothing is going to change me,' she answered briskly, thinking that was the way to go. 'And that's fine about Jili and Jacob. No problem!' How could she say that, when the piece of news had had a tremendous impact on her? They would be quite alone. And he had planned it that way.

'Then why are you looking so unnerved?' He tucked a stray raven lock behind her ear.

'Well, it *was* kind of a bolt from the blue, Bryn.' She turned to slide into the waiting vehicle. 'I wish I could tell you otherwise, but I'm not much of a cook,' she tacked on when he was behind the wheel.

His laugh came from deep in his throat. 'It was never your cooking skills, Francey, that attracted my attention.'

She belted herself in, and then smoothed back her long hair, giving herself time to settle. 'I didn't know I had.'

'That is just so untrue, Francey,' he mocked. 'Quite beneath you, in fact. We've always had a connection.' He turned on the ignition. 'God, it's good to be back. It's a magnificent day.'

'It is indeed!' The air was so pure, so dry, so bush

aromatic—and the space and the freedom! It was like no place else. And, let's face it, she was thrilled to the core to be sharing these precious days with him. Separate rooms? She could feel the yearning that was in her shooting off her like sparks.

'Jili will have left plenty of food for us,' he was saying. 'We'll have lunch. Go for a drive around the main areas. Check everything out. Catch up with the men. I'm not all that happy about Roy Forster staying on as overseer.' He cast her a questioning glance.

'Me either,' Francesca said. 'Forster was Grandfather's choice. A real yes-man. Jacob would be a better choice for the job. Roy pretty much relies on Jacob anyway. But how do we go about demoting Roy? I wouldn't want to sack him. He's competent enough—'

'But not the right man for the job,' Bryn finished off for her. 'What about if we shift him to one of the other stations, say Kurrawana in the Gulf?'

'You've thought about it?'

'Yes.'

'He mightn't want to go.'

'On the other hand he might jump at it. Let me handle it,' Bryn said.

'Yes, boss.' A little dryness escaped her, when in reality she was in awe of his many skills, all of which he had mastered. Everything Bryn did was done not only with the highest level of compe- tence, but with considerable flair.

'You don't like that idea?' A black brow shot up.

She slanted him a smile. 'What? You calling the shots? Only teasing, Bryn—though you *do* give orders to the manner born. Grandfather wanted you to run the whole operation.'

'You'll be consulted all along the way. That's a promise. No decision will be made without your approval. I won't take anything on alone.'

'That's great to know. But I trust you, Bryn. I know you'll be working hard to bring Daramba back to what it was. It has deteriorated a bit.'

'It will be a whole different story when Jacob takes over,' Bryn said.

The hours were passing far too swiftly for Francesca. It was a marvellous experience to be with Bryn. They both had quick, curious minds, both were keenly observant, so they were able to spend the afternoon in stimulating discussion. It was uncanny, really, the way they kept arriving at the same conclusions.

Francesca took great satisfaction from the fact that Bryn listened carefully to every suggestion she had to make. And most of them he seemed prepared to take on board. It occurred to her in hindsight that on those rare occasions when she had got into discussion with her grandfather he had listened too. How odd to think of that now. But, unlike her grandfather, Bryn's manner with the station staff was relaxed and friendly. She could see how well they responded to it, without ever overstepping the line. Never in all the years had any member of her family joined the men for their tea break, but she and Bryn did so now, enjoying the smoky billy tea and the freshly baked damper that the men had liberally smeared with home-made rosella jam or bush honey.

There was a new stockman in the team, Vance Bormann, a big man, bulky on top but by no means overweight, more like a prize fighter, with a swarthy face, weathered skin and a full, macho-looking moustache. He wore his battered black Akubra low over heavy-lidded dark eyes. Roy Forster had taken him on only a few weeks back. The general opinion was the man was good at his job. Francesca, on the other hand, was none too sure she liked the look of him—a woman's opinion? In fact she had a vague feeling she had seen him some place before. She couldn't for the life of her think where or when. Maybe he reminded her of some cowboy in the old Westerns? The guy who was always the baddie.

She found herself sitting in court, surrounded by station employees she had known for years, talking in particular to one of the stockmen she had favoured from childhood. Taree Newton—part aboriginal, his hair now a mass of pure white curls—was a man who could handle any animal on the station and fix any piece of machinery, and he could tell wonderful stories of the Dreamtime and 'other-world' matters, some of which as a child she had found deliciously scary.

'Catch up with me, little'un,' Taree used to call to her as she tagged after him. 'Catch up with me.' Taree, her guardian angel. He had always been on the move, with a string of jobs to do. 'Plenty a work, Missy Francey. Too much work.' But he had always found time for her, keeping the keenest eye on her. Aunt Elizabeth had used to call Taree 'Francey's nanny'.

She noticed Bryn had taken Roy Forster aside, no doubt to discuss Roy's future. There would always be a place for Roy within the pastoral chain, but unquestionably Jacob would fill the role of overseer here a good deal better. Jili would be thrilled! She glanced up to catch Vance Bormann staring at her. She had the impression he had been observing her long and hard. He was very much a stranger, for all her feeling that she had sighted him before. When he realised she was aware of his staring, he swiftly rose from where he had been sitting, going back through the trees as if he were ready to continue work. It wasn't unnatural for a man to stare at a woman. She had received plenty of attention from the male sex for years now. But this was the first time she had thought there was something sinister about it. Surely not? If she mentioned it to Bryn she knew the likely consequence would be the man would be out of a job. Maybe it was his rather unfortunate looks? But wasn't it unfair judging a book by its cover?

Late afternoon, as the heat of the blazing sun was abating, they took the horses out. She a glossy-flanked liver-chestnut mare called Jalilah; he a big black gelding, Cosmo, with a white blaze and white socks—both ex-racehorses, alert and very fast when underway.

Francesca's face shone with pleasure. She had so missed not being able to go for a ride. Now she revelled in the scent of horseflesh, the scent of leather, the scent of the still blossoming bush. Bryn rode close beside her, his hands easy on the reins. He was an experienced rider, as she was, though both of them knew he would always beat her in a race. Initially the horses were restless—Jalilah particularly skittish, having been cooped up for too long—so once away from the home compound and out onto the flats they gave the horses their heads.

Manes and tails streamed like pennants in the wind as they headed out to the first line of billabongs. Sunset wasn't that far off. Afterwards the world would swiftly turn from delicate mauve to pitch-black. They would need to be back within the compound by then.

Not far from their destination the mare, high-strung at the best of times, was spooked by a pair of wallabies that shot up out of nowhere and then bounded away. The mare reared, forelegs folded up under her, but Francesca, leg and thigh muscles working, got her quickly under control, to the point where the mare steadied, dancing nervily on the highly coloured red sand laced with water-storing pink *parakeelya,* and the bright green spinifex that would soon turn to a scorched gold.

The hills in the distance that had appeared so solid and so glowing a red at noon now appeared to be floating free of the ground, their bases disguised by the thick silver-grey mist formed by condensation from the many rock pools. Without so much as a word to the other, in silent communication they rode down on Kala-Guli Creek, the prettiest and most secluded spring-fed pool on the entire station. Unless one knew exactly where to find Kala-Guli, any visitor unfamiliar with the vast landscape could ride on unawares. Not all of these beautiful hidden pools, however, were safe. Many a poor beast had been sucked in and lost for ever in the quicksand that often lurked where there was plenty of underground water.

It had been suggested at one time that was the way Gulla Nolan had disappeared, but those who had known Gulla refused point-blank to go along with the theory. Gulla had known this country like the back of his hand. If Gulla had been sucked into quicksand he would have been dragged there, hands and feet tightly bound. At various times over the years Francesca had fancied she'd heard Gulla's cries of terror, amplified by the desert wind. But then, as Carina had frequently told her scornfully, she had way too much imagination.

White cockatoos appeared in magic droves, settling like winged angels in the trees. Bryn and Francesca dismounted, tethered their horses, stretched their limbs, then walked down towards the waterline, with bushy ferns and brittle ground cover grasses snagging the hems of their jeans. Butterflies of many colours, beautiful to the eye, drifted about like petals, luminous when slanting rays of sunlight caught their wings. Francesca trailed a hand over a native honeysuckle, a brilliant yellow with a honeysuckle's true perfume. The creek was several feet below the level of the plain throughout its course. Here the heated air off the grasslands turned balmy, perfumed with the scent of hundreds and hundreds of wild lilies, purple in colour, which grew in profusion along the banks of the long, narrow stream. It was enormously refreshing after the dazzling power of the sun.

'Man finds his true home in nature,' Bryn commented, lending a hand to her as they moved down a fairly steep and slippery slope.

'I suppose that's where we're closest to God.'

He gave her a half-smile, feeling a profound

tenderness for her and her strong spiritual beliefs. 'Do you ever pray for me, Francey?' he asked.

Of course she prayed for him. He was so very special to her. 'What do you think?' she replied, eyes sparkling.

'I think I may be in need of it.' He tightened his hold on her as they moved further down the bank, where little wildflowers similar to pansies showed their velvety faces.

'Me too,' she said, and it wasn't banter.

And there were the moss-covered rocks of various shapes and sizes she so loved and had often sketched. Some, shelf-like, jutted out into the water, forming a natural sunbathing area. How they had used it when they were young! Only now the feathery acacias fanned right out over the creek from both sides, dipping in low arches like weeping willows, their branches cascading to within touching distance. Here too a white mist hung low, like a smoky haze over the stream for as far as they could see. By the time they stood on the golden stretch of dry sand a flock of finches had zoomed down over the water, drinking their fill, then rising in a whirr of tiny wings. It all added to the extraordinary fascination of the place.

'This is exquisite, isn't it?' she breathed quietly, letting the fresh coolness get to her and her heated skin. The creek was completely deserted, except for them and the colonies of birds. Brilliant little lorikeets, rising flashes of sapphire, ruby and emerald, darted and wheeled through the branches above them. 'It looks like it has been here since the beginning of time.'

For answer, Bryn began to unbutton his shirt. 'Let's take a quick dip,' he suggested. 'It looks so darn inviting.'

She drew in her breath sharply, her whole body tensing, the lower half of her body flooded with sexual heat like spiralling little flames. 'Are you serious?'

'Of course I'm serious,' he said, stripping off his shirt and regarding her with amusement. 'God, Francey, we've taken a dip here countless times over the years.'

'I'd need my swimsuit first.'

'Oh, come off it,' he mocked. 'Strip down to your bra and briefs. I bet they're more respectable than most bikinis on the beach.'

She watched him, dry-mouthed, unzip his jeans and then step out of them, very comfortable with it. All that was left to cover his superb male body was a pair of navy briefs that clung low on his hips. There wasn't a skerrick of excess flesh on him. She couldn't seem to tear her eyes away from his sculpted body, nor control her eyes' descent. She could feel her cheeks flush. She could hear the beat of her heart.

'I don't know that I want to take off my clothes,' she said, her voice trailing off uncertainly. She was just so modest. Maybe too modest—and no one made her feel more acutely conscious of her own body than Bryn.

'Excuse me,' he corrected, suddenly looking up at her, 'you *do*. It'll cool you down. Come on, girl! I'm not going to drown you, if that's what you're wondering.'

His mockery fired her up. 'Okay. Turn your back until I'm in the water.'

'Francey, you amaze me—but okay.' His voice was languid, lazy, taunting. He stood studying her for a moment longer, then stepped up onto a flat-topped rock that jutted out into the deep water and dived off it, surfacing a moment later, with water streaming off his jet-black hair, his face and wide shoulders, the hard muscle of his gleaming upper torso. 'The water's great. Come on!' He beckoned to her, much as he had done through all the years of her childhood. He only had to beckon and she followed.

Quickly she looked around her. Plenty of branches from which to hang her clothes—a sapphire-blue tank top and her jeans. She was already out of her riding boots. She turned away, hearing the sound of Bryn's splashing. Damn him! If she were Carrie she'd have had all her clothes off in less than a minute. Carrie was quite comfortable with nudity. She had a great body. Not that there was anything wrong with Francesca's own body. Nothing wrong with her underwear either. She liked good lingerie. Her bra was silk, with matching briefs, pale pink, patterned with violet and blue flowers and tiny red hearts. All quite respectable. Maybe he wouldn't notice the hearts.

Just as she reached the water, dipping in an exploratory toe, he shocked her by surfacing in the middle of the pool, treading water while he stared at her with open delight.

'You look exquisite!' he called out. 'If I were gifted, like you, I'd depict you as a mythical water nymph—say, Ondine. But naked, of course. Nakedness absolutely obligatory. Either emerging from the depths of the pool, or perhaps lying stretched out on that rock shelf over there, with flowers in your long hair. Either one would work.'

She saw his eyes linger on her small, high breasts, then slowly and deliberately move down her body to her legs. 'Sounds pretty erotic!' She was panicked, but felt a strange desire to stay exactly where she was, with his eyes on her.

'Eros should be your middle name!'

'Now, that's bizarre!' she protested. He couldn't be serious. Just having a bit of fun. She had never seen herself as an erotic being, unaware that many people described her as intensely alluring. 'Carrie is the exhibitionist,' she said, for once accurately nailing her cousin. 'But you already know that.'

'Well, actually I *do!* But that's an entirely different thing.'

What wouldn't he know about Carrie after their affair? And according to Carrie the sexual intrigue continued. She didn't want to believe that. Bryn had denied it. But the niggling thought remained that Carrie would always be there before her.

'Stand there a moment longer, can't you?' he called 'You know your body is perfectly proportioned, like the ideal dancer's? Neck to waist, to hip, to knee, to ankle.'

'Got a tape measure, have you?' She made very

slow progress into the emerald-green pool waters, some part of her revelling in his frank stare.

'I have a really good eye.'

'I know that.' She felt as if he was slowly peeling what little she still wore off her. It was like being held in golden chains. Bound to him. More like a wildly shy adolescent than a grown woman, she plunged in, striking out without hesitation. The water was surprisingly cold at first, but all the more energising for that. She was a good swimmer, fast over short distances. Naturally he was stronger. He caught her in the middle of the pool, though she pretended to duck away.

It didn't make one scrap of difference. He had her.

Bryn experienced the searing realisation that his hands had taken on a life of their own. He pushed the straps of her bra down over her shoulders, revealing the tender upper curves of her breasts and the half-hidden rosebud nipples.

It was an enormous shock and an enormous excitation. Francesca's heart worked its way into her throat.

'You know what you are?' His voice was intense.

'Show me.'

She couldn't control it. Yearning burst from her,

sweeping her away. Within seconds it had demolished the dam of loneliness that had been built up over the years, leaving in its wake a great curling wave of emotion. She felt transcendent, ready for his kiss, which came the instant he had her locked in his arms.

'Francey!' He took the sweet mouth that opened to him. Took it hungrily. His tongue reached into the moist cavern, its tip teasing her. It was glorious, the press of flesh against flesh. A delirium of pleasure. The softness of her now naked breasts against the taut plain of his torso. Heart of one thudding into the other.

They went under, neither of them drawing back, bobbed up against each other, gasping, then slowly sinking, their mouths locked, her long, slender legs hooked around his. She wasn't going to lose this one chance. She would show him she was a woman. Not the hesitant and fearful girl he had watched growing up.

Surfacing again, he took her long wet rope of hair in his hands, drawing her to him more roughly than he'd intended—but he was thoroughly aroused. How could he not be? He had waited so long for her, taken her in his imagination. She looked impossibly beautiful, with water coursing over her, the thick mane of her hair a sleek ribbon down her back, her great luminous eyes tinged with the green of the overhanging trees.

'This is dangerous what we're doing, isn't it?' she whispered to him, even though the light in her eyes was urging him on. 'Reckless. And it was *your* idea.'

He held her hard at the waist, fusing their lower bodies so she could not be unaware of his powerful arousal. For him there was only Francesca. No one else. Her skin in the dappled sunlight was perfection, beaded with tiny sprays of diamonds.

'Why didn't I think of it long before this?' Of course he *had* thought of it, *dreamed* of it, so many times—but Carina had made it her business never to leave them alone together. 'Francesca, you beautiful creature!' he groaned, aware his strong hands on her were beginning to tremble faintly—a sure sign of his monumental desire. The waiting had been impossibly long.

Francesca found her eyelids dropping heavily, her eyes filled with tears. His voice was so warm, so deep, so desiring. Voices were wonderful instruments of seduction. Voices were weapons.

'You're not crying? Francey?' Concern washed

over him, and his driving passion was forced to take a step backwards. 'What is it? Tell me,' he urged.

'Tears come easily to me,' she murmured shakily, placing her hand against the tangle of black hair on his chest that had tightened into whorls.

'Why?'

'Pain is never far behind pleasure.' She stared up into his eyes, black as night.

'You think that will happen if we make love?' God knew he didn't think he had any reserve of control left. His sex felt rigid, rock-hard. He was desperate to plunge into her. It was *pain* he suffered, however sublime.

Her thoughts had turned chaotic. Indeed, she sometimes thought her whole existence had been chaotic. Once he made love to her all the secrets of her life would be unlocked. He would know her so intimately. She would have handed over the larger part of herself. Wouldn't it be far safer for a woman if the man was more in love with her than she with him? There was always one who kissed and one who turned the cheek. Great love unreciprocated at the same level could be a disaster. Didn't she have Carrie for a role model?

It's part of his plan. Didn't I tell you?

Out of nowhere Francesca heard her cousin's

voice. It was so piercingly clear she even looked swiftly over her shoulder, as though Carina might be standing on the stretch of sand, watching them locked in their watery embrace. Though she was desperate for Bryn to carry her back to the shore, to expose her naked body to his eyes, to reach deep into her yearning body with his own, to claim what was his, fear suddenly overtook her whole person. Carina's warning words rose up like a curse to haunt her.

He'll be everything you ever wanted or wished for, but there'll be a price to pay.

Life had taught her that was cruelly true. She wasn't equal to the power and skill of this beautiful man. Even half submerged in cold lake water his hungry clasp heated her blood. He touched her to her very soul. Didn't that make her his slave? Had his *bid* for her—could she possibly see it as Carina had warned?—come too fast? Here in this enchanted place he knew she would be totally under his spell. It was in the very nature of the man-woman relationship.

Before her body could further betray her, she threw her arms adroitly back over her head, her body half lifting out of the water as she swam a few butterfly strokes away from him.

'Can we stop now, Bryn?' she begged, when she was a distance off. Her insecurities were starkly on show and there was nothing she could do about it. Soaring hearts could just as well fall and be broken. She wrenched the sodden silk bra that encircled her waist back into position, sleekly encasing her breasts. She might be a woman, but she was still frozen in time.

He gave a quick frown. 'Of course.' It wasn't just physical lust that drove him—the need to possess her. He *loved* her. But he could see she was having the fiercest struggle with her emotions. Something was desperately ailing her. But what? She had to be ready for him. He wasn't prepared to force her to overcome her fears, though he knew he could. 'You're always safe with me, Francey. Remember that. Anyway, it's getting late.' He thrust one hand through his glistening raven hair. 'The sun will set soon.'

She rapidly calmed at his tone. What was he thinking? That nothing was ever going to change Francey? 'Let's have our swim first,' she suggested, her voice warm and sweet with conciliation.

He swam up beside her, no hint of bruised male ego in his voice or on his dynamic face. 'I tell you what!' he said, as though she was back to half her age. 'The last one to reach that big moss-mottled rock up there jutting out into the water makes dinner.'

Her heart lifted in a kind of relief. She couldn't bear to have Bryn angry and disappointed in her. 'You're on! Just give me a start.'

'Not *too* much of one,' he scoffed. 'You're fast in short bursts. All right—go!' His voice rang out in that beautiful, secluded place. It startled the parrots. They rose in a vivid rainbow wave, then flew off, protesting, to more distant trees.

CHAPTER SIX

SHE had almost finished dressing. Paradoxically, she had dressed herself up as a woman might for the man she loved. Now she sat in front of the dressing table, staring sightlessly at her own image, as captured fragments of the afternoon came back to haunt her. Or more accurately to *taunt* her. She had been over and over her behaviour of the afternoon, and the causes for it. She wanted to hold on to those lingering sensations of rapture when she had been so magically transformed, but her sharp withdrawal from Bryn's embrace, her renouncement of bliss, kept interfering. How easy it was to lose one's way! She had blown her chance, maybe her *only* chance.

A deeply entrenched habit of hers, her mind resorted to Shakespeare. *'There is a tide in the affairs of men—'*and presumably women? *'—which when taken at the flood leads on to fortune. Omitted, all the voyage of their life, is bound in shallows and in miseries...'*

Who was going to argue with arguably the greatest literary genius in the history of mankind, with his sublime understanding of human nature and the power to express it? If she had missed the tide, then maybe she deserved it. Fortune favoured the brave. Fear was her weakness. She had to break free of it, haul herself up. Now Bryn had reverted to the easy companionship of her childhood and adolescence, apparently accepting she was harbouring myriad anxieties. The pounding passion of that episode in the water might not have happened. It was just one of her daydreams that went on for hours.

Slowly she drew her hairbrush through the rippling length of her long hair, listening to its electric crackle. It reminded her of the times when Aunt Elizabeth had brushed her hair as a child. They had been very close. Far closer than her own blood. Satisfied with the result, she set the brush down, giving vent to a sigh.

'The arrow of time flies in only one direction.' Some other genius had said that. She had an idea it was Einstein. Einstein would no doubt have gone on to point out the enormous pulling power of the past and its impact on the future. But in the end one could only go *forwards*. Not backwards.

She *had* to win. Mostly she did, but it had to be *all* the time. Carina pushed gamesmanship to the limit. Wasn't it highly unlikely, then, that Carina had accepted the loss of the man she intensely desired? With all Francesca knew of her cousin, Carina would be most likely to covet what she knew she could never possess. She might be forced to accept Bryn was never going to ask her to marry him, but Francesca couldn't see Carina surrendering him to any other woman. And the worst possible scenario would be to a woman like herself.

Carina's jealousy over Elizabeth's affection for her had just about ruined their childhood. Of course Carina had so often played the caricature of the loving, caring older cousin, but she had never felt it had been real. Carina's genius was for fooling people, confusing them, hiding behind an elaborate mask.

The issue of Bryn remained unresolved.

Yesterday, when Carina had come into the office, she had forced on herself a particular role. But what had she hoped to achieve by doing so? A cessation of hostilities, even though the hostilities had been all one-sided? What had she been playing at when she'd insisted she was only looking out for Francesca's interests? When had

Carina *ever* looked out for her? Her mind had all but shut down on that traumatic incident of their childhood when she had almost drowned, only for Bryn's miraculous intervention, with Carina standing by screaming...and screaming...as though she had never wanted any of it to happen.

Even now, all these years later, she couldn't bear to think it had been anything other than an accident that could always happen when children were left unattended. Only sometimes in the realm of her dreams she relived that day... The walk along the banks of the lagoon hand in hand, which had come as a lovely surprise, her exclaiming over the beauty of the waterlilies, how she was going to draw them the minute she was home, her scrapbook in her hand... Carina had hated the way she was always drawing... She remembered the danger of the deep water...the way Carina had waded in, which meant she'd had to go too. It was the paralysing feeling of extreme danger that always forced her awake.

What *had* happened that day? Would she find the answer in her dreams if only she could let the nightmare run its course? Would she have that dream for ever? Her lungs bursting...her hands locked around thirteen-year-old Bryn's neck as he waded out, carrying her in his strong young arms. She remembered looking down at the waist-deep water, and then they were safely on the sand. She must have been near choking him, clinging to him the way she had, though he'd told her afterwards she'd weighed no more than a feather. She remembered he'd had algae caught in his thick, gleaming thatch of hair. Lurid green against black. She remembered she hadn't cried. She had been trying so hard to be brave. A look of bewilderment crossed her face—hadn't she whispered something in his ear? It had to have been a secret, but she couldn't remember it.

All she did remember was that Bryn had rescued her as if he'd been sent by the Great Spirit of the Bush. She believed in such spirits, as the aboriginal people did. They moved across the earth, always standing by to give aid to the chosen, though they remained for the most part invisible. Even Bryn, the sanest man she knew, acknowledged the spirits of the Timeless Land and what they could do.

She was ready to go downstairs, still fighting off her demons. Reaching for a pair of silver bracelets, she slipped them on like an amulet. She was wearing one of her new semi-casual dresses for evening. Adele Bennett had picked it out for her. Adele certainly knew what she liked and what suited her. This particular dress was ankle-length, the material a gauzy water colour silk-chiffon. Very Ondine-ish, she thought with a smile.

The dress had a beautiful belt to go with it. Another one of Adele's finds. It curved snugly around the waist, then dipped low in front, elongating her torso. The belt had a gorgeous enamelled clasp, made up like a large open-faced flower, violet in colour, with a yellow centre and petals dotted with deep pink crystals like dewdrops. Lime-green and turquoise butterflies, their wings similarly encrusted, alighted on either side. It was a work of art in itself. A beautiful dress wasn't just a flattering garment that made a woman feel special. A beautiful dress was more like a magic talisman. Great things could happen! This dress would protect her. It had already given her waning confidence a boost.

So much depended not on Bryn, but on *her*. She had been a hair's breadth away from letting him make love to her. She didn't think he would tolerate a rebuff like that again. Rapture turned on, then abruptly turned off? The last thing she wanted was to have a sense of strain between them. Life wasn't a game. Love was to be taken very seriously. It was the one thing that really mattered.

Needless to say, Bryn had let her win their race—though it must have been hard—and now it was his job to get dinner. She had told him she was no cook just for something to say. She was, in fact, a good cook and proud of it—she had taken courses as part of her education—so she was ready to help out. That was if she was needed. Bryn had always been great at barbecues. A funny thing, the way men liked to take over at barbecues, if nowhere else…

'S-o-o-o!' he murmured on a long drawn-out breath as he turned to face her. 'That's an extraordinarily beautiful dress. Very romantic.'

He dazzled her with the blaze in his eyes. She responded with a low curtsy. 'Glad you like it.'

'Your eyes are more violet than grey tonight. They've picked up one of the colours in the dress. It amazes me when that happens.'

'What happens?' She leaned towards him, giving a funny little theatrical blink.

'The way your eyes change colour.' He let his gaze rove over her, from her lustrous hair to her silver-sandal-shod feet. 'Large eyes. Your eyes and your arching brows dominate your face in the way of certain women icons. Callas, Loren, and of course Audrey Hepburn.'

'The Big League?' She smiled, conscious of the excited pulses that had started up in her body.

She moved further into the mammoth room, with its custom-made cabinetry, black and white marble-tiled floor, marble benchtops and marble-topped islands. Stainless steel pots and pans hung from a stainless steel fitting suspended from the ceiling. The kitchen had been fitted out with every conceivable appliance. Just for the hell of it, she supposed. Only now and again had her grandfather entertained here. Mostly he'd kept well away from his flagship station.

'I'm expecting a really good dinner,' she warned Bryn. 'This afternoon's ride has made me hungry.' She kept her voice light. 'So what's on the menu? Do you need any help?'

He shot her a droll glance. 'Francey, I understood you to say you couldn't find your way around a kitchen?'

'I was never allowed in one,' she confessed with regret, picking up the bottle of chilled white wine that sat opened on the bench and pouring a pale greenish-gold stream into an empty waiting glass.

'Here—I should have done that,' he said, laying down his knife. He had been chopping fresh herbs, releasing wonderfully pungent aromas.

'That's okay. You're busy. I like that. You know the way we lived,' she said, sipping the wine, catching the fragrance of lime blossom. She broke off with a delighted comment. 'This is delicious. It's got quite a snap to it. I prefer a good Riesling over a Chardonnay.'

'That's why I opened it,' he said. Francesca was no drinker, but she had a fine palate. 'I know you and Carrie lived like little princesses.' He made a clicking sound with his tongue. 'Even if you *were* the little princess in the tower.'

'I'd much rather have been treated like a normal person.'

'Only it didn't happen that way. Poor Francey!'

'That's why I took a couple of cookery courses— just in case I got married and my husband expected me to be able to turn out a good meal.'

'Do you think you'd ever have to?' he asked drolly, midnight-dark eyes mocking. 'You're the Forsyth heiress, Francesca, like it or not.'

'And you're the Macallan heir,' she shot back. 'I mean, *you* haven't had a normal life either.'

'True. But I suppose it's normal enough for me. We've been given a lot, Francey. We have to be able to take the good with the bad. Speaking of the good—we're having cucumber rounds with Tasmanian smoked salmon for starters. No, don't interrupt. I found the horseradish cream and the capers after a lengthy search, when they were right in front of me. Jili has left fresh herbs from her garden, as you see: parsley, mint, basil. There are a few others in the crisper. Beef fillet with mushrooms to follow, and there's a chocolate mousse I've taken out of the freezer and put in the fridge about fifteen minutes ago. Jili whipped it up for us before she left.'

'Good for Jili!' she exclaimed. 'Now, Jili really *is* a good cook. But don't let that put you off,' she added with mock kindness. 'So where are we going to eat? I don't like it in here. You could seat an army and still have room for reinforcements.'

'Sir Francis always thought big,' Bryn remarked dryly. 'He was notorious for it. What about—?'

'I know,' she broke in. 'The Palm Room. It's about the only room I like.'

'You took the words right out of my mouth,'

Bryn said, twisting the top off a jar of capers. 'You could set the table. You *can* do that?'

'Very funny!' She was feeling so extraordinarily light hearted she felt she could soar.

Francesca found she was every bit as hungry as she'd claimed. The starter was just right—light and crunchy, the richness of the smoked salmon cut by the cucumber, the horseradish sauce and a sprinkle of lemon. The Daramba beef fillet simply melted in the mouth, as did the selection of mushrooms, and Jili's chocolate mousse was flavoured with Amaretto liqueur. Bryn scooped it out like ice cream and dusted it with cocoa powder. His own touch.

'Perfect!' Francesca enthused, laying down her dessert spoon. 'Let me make the coffee.'

'No, sit there.' He shook his head, rising to his feet. 'I'm enjoying showing off.'

'You don't want it to get around how good you are at turning out a meal,' she warned him. 'You'll have to fight off complete strangers.'

'I take it you mean women?' he asked suavely over his shoulder.

'Of course women. God, don't give me a heart attack. As it is your female admirers stretch for miles.'

He didn't deny it. 'Amazing when all I need and want is one.'

Over the beef fillet they had abandoned white wine for red. Picking up her crystal wine glass, Francesca leaned back in her bamboo armchair. The chair was comfortably upholstered in a fabric she liked—an embossed damask in a deep shade of crimson that stood up to all the greenery in the room, the luxuriant palms and tree ferns in their huge pots, and the dark timbers of the Asian furnishings. Smiling dreamily to herself, she drank a little more of the Margaret River Cabernet Sauvignon. It was from their own state of Western Australia, the ruggedly beautiful Margaret River wine region, which had fast become one of the world's viticulture hot spots. This red she loved. It was smooth and elegant, with a succulent blackcurrant flavour.

After the drama of the afternoon, the night was a dream. A huge full moon saturated the enormous panorama of Daramba in its radiance. Through the floor-to-ceiling doors that stood open to the rear terrace the night wind came in deliciously cool gusts, spiked with the native boronia that grew wild. Which brought her to thinking of a garden. She would have to do something about establishing one. Bring in a landscaper capable of turning the desert site into an oasis. Jili had her extensive vegetable garden, which flourished. Her grandfather hadn't minded that. The produce was used in the house and around the station. But he hadn't shown the slightest interest in establishing a garden, either at the Forsyth mausoleum or at Daramba homestead. Didn't that say something about the aridity of his character? It wasn't as though he hadn't been able to spare the money, though she realised it would take a lot. Gardens just hadn't been in his philosophy.

The success of an Outback garden was going to depend on the skill of the landscaper and his ability to choose plants that would thrive in the dry. She had her heart set on date palms—as advanced as could be obtained and successfully transplanted. And she wanted a large water garden. Daramba abounded in underground springs. The University of Western Australia had a magnificent campus of more than fifty hectares, set in a superb natural bush setting. She had always loved the Canary Island date palms in the grounds there. Her home state was dry, yet beautiful gardens flourished. Why not here? She just needed the right person to handle the job. Lady

Macallan could help her there. She was something of an authority on gardens. She adored her own magnificent garden, which was open to public viewing at certain times of the year.

'What are you thinking about?' Bryn asked as he wheeled in the trolley.

'Gardens,' she said, turning her jewelled gaze on him.

Bryn smiled with satisfaction. 'I knew you'd get around to it. The homestead is crying out for a proper setting. So too is the family mansion, but Charles and Carrie seem happy enough with the way it is. You need a home of your own, you know, Francey. You weren't left the mansion.'

'Thank God!' She sighed with feel feeling. 'It's such a strange place. More like a public building. Take those monumental pilasters supporting roaring lions at the front gate. What was *with* Grandfather and lions, do you know?'

'Wasn't Leo his star sign?' Bryn poured coffee, placing one in front of her. 'He named one of his sons Lionel. Sir Frank and my grandfather visited South Africa in their youth. They were stationed in Cape Town with friends, but they travelled quite extensively. It's a wonder he didn't try to bag a lion and bring it home.'

'What—shoot it?' she cried, horrified.

Bryn laughed and shook his head. 'No, he'd have liked nothing better than to capture it live, bring it back, then let it wander around the grounds of the family home. You know—start a tradition.'

'At least that's better than shooting such a splendid creature. I plan on asking Lady Macallan's advice regarding a landscaper for here. I want date palms. Lots of them. Desert oaks. Native plants. A big water garden. God knows we've got plenty of room.'

'I'm sure she'll be delighted to help you,' Bryn said.

After coffee he allowed her to help him. Then, when the kitchen had been returned to its immaculate condition and the dishes stacked away, they decided on a short walk.

'Even if it's only around the driveway.' Bryn spoke lightly, though he was acutely aware of his soaring sensory perceptions. As always with Francesca—holding her hand guaranteed sexual arousal. 'Do you remember the stone fountain that used to grace the centre of the driveway when the Frazers used to own it?' he asked, striving for the casual. She was wearing that lovely elusive perfume he always associated with her, and it was really getting to him. 'I don't suppose you do. You were too young.'

'My father and Grandfather were already estranged.'

'Yes,' he acknowledged. 'I wonder what happened to the fountain? The Frazers had it sent out from Italy. Three winged horses supported the main basin with rearing front legs. I think my grandfather tried to find out where it had gone, but Frank was very non-committal. I wouldn't be in the least surprised if he had it reduced to rubble.'

'Oh, surely not?' she cried, dismayed.

'Don't take it personally.'

'How can I not take it personally? Sir Francis was my grandfather.'

'That doesn't make him a saint, Francey,' Bryn said bluntly. 'But better late than never. He left the Forsyth fortune largely in your hands.'

She stared up at his handsome, chiselled profile, gilded by the exterior lights. 'You know what I've been thinking about?'

Going to bed with me? Bryn was in half-agony, half-rapture. How the hell was he going to get through the night without her beside him?

'Couldn't we return one of the Queensland

stations, say Mount Kolah, to being a wildlife area?' she suggested persuasively. 'I understand it has quite a few protected species within its boundaries.'

Bryn stopped in his tracks. 'You've been talking to someone from the Bush Heritage Authority?'

'Ross Fitzgibbon. But he certainly didn't suggest it.'

'Ha!' said Bryn, and walked on.

'He *didn't!*'

'Francey, Ross Fitzgibbon spends his *life* spreading the message.'

'Why wouldn't he? He's one of our leading ecologists.'

'We can talk about this,' Bryn said, meaning it, 'but not tonight. I just want to relax. Last I heard they were having trouble on Mount Kolah from feral pigs. As far as that goes, Roy Forster told me they might have to organise a hunt here, for the leader of a dingo pack that hangs out on the desert fringe. It seems the brute has acquired a taste for blood, savaging calves. It's more dangerous than a pure-bred dingo because it has German Shepherd blood in it. Not from a station dog. Some desert traveller either lost a dog or abandoned it. This isn't the city. Out here it's primeval power that reigns. We'll never tame it.'

They were rounding the side of the homestead, out of the broad reach of the exterior lights and their excessive brightness. Unknown to them they were walking towards a dark figure who had broken all the rules by entering the home compound and then, seeing them emerge from the house, swiftly withdrawn to a hiding place behind the stone archway that led to the vegetable and fruit gardens.

He couldn't make out what they were saying, and his hearing was razor-sharp. Their bodies had drawn close together. He warned himself to be careful. The man was the danger. The woman would present no problem. That was what he'd been told. By the Bitch—that was how he thought of her—who had treated him like scum, instead of as a trained professional whose expertise was unquestioned. Yet she was only too pleased to hire him to carry out her dirty work—like her grandfather before her.

He'd been furious when he'd first found out she knew all about him, what he had done for the Iron Man, how to contact him. He'd thought of it as blowing his cover. Where had she got her information from? He couldn't accept it was from the old man. Forsyth had known better than anyone how to cover his tracks. The Bitch had the same piercing blue eyes that seemed to see right through you. She was a real stunner, but he hated her. Hated her sort. A normal woman would think what she was asking him to do too monstrous to even put into words. Not her!

It hadn't taken him any time at all to land a job on the station and settle in. There weren't many jobs he couldn't handle. He had grown up on a small Outback cattle run, with a father who had beaten the hell out of him and his mother. He'd done what he had to do. He'd joined the army. Served in the world's trouble spots. That was where he had learned how to take care of business. These days he was more of a mercenary—bodyguard, security man, enforcer, contract guy.

Although he was a man of violence, he didn't like hurting women. Especially not one who looked like a Madonna. He had always stopped short of that. But the Bitch had too much on him, and she had only contempt for his fearsome reputation. Her grandfather had raised her in his image. He had to bide his time. He was in. An opportunity would arise. He felt a surge of rebellion. He didn't like it. He didn't like being dictated to by a woman—a woman, moreover, as ruthless as any enemy he had faced. The only good thing—if one could call it that—was that the Madonna wouldn't feel a thing...

Francesca thought she saw a blur out of the corner of her eye. It unnerved her. 'I'd like to go back now, Bryn,' she said quietly.

'Of course.' He caught the anxious note in her voice. 'Is anything wrong?' She had clutched his hand, as though to have him with her was everything.

'No. I just have an odd feeling we're being watched.'

'What?' Bryn jerked his head in the only direction there was cover. 'I'm sure there's no one about, Francey. None of the men would come up to the house at this time of night unless there was an emergency. They would identify themselves, anyway.'

'I know that.' Still she was caught fast in tendrils of panic.

'I'll take you back to the house, then I'll have a look around.' Bryn drew her closer to his side. 'It's moonlight. There's very little cover except for Jili's vegetable garden,' he pointed out. 'Perhaps it's being raided by a bird? Stand on the path and wait. I'll take a look.'

'No!' Her breath shuddered. 'It's like Carrie always says—I have too much imagination.'

'I'll check all the same,' he said.

'Be careful.' Vivid imagination or not, she was certain her internal radar had picked up some signal. Her heart beating hard, she waited for Bryn to return.

'Nothing,' he said, but he was not absolutely sure she hadn't picked up something. Francesca, even as a child, had had an extra sense.

They were back in the house. He checked all the doors on the ground floor, making it appear like a normal nightly ritual. No unauthorised person had ever dared invade the Forsyth privacy. No member of staff would arrive at the homestead unannounced. The men were all known to him, with the exception of the new guy, the big, burly Vance Bormann. He had questioned Roy Forster about the new arrival, but Roy had assured him Bormann checked out. Maybe it had been Gulla Nolan's ghost hanging around? There were many legends woven around Gulla. Maybe he was keeping an eye on the place?

'All right to go to bed,' he said, turning to face

her. It wasn't meant as a question—though God knew he wanted it to be. Her beautiful eyes were like saucers, the black pupils enlarged. 'I'll take the bedroom opposite instead of down the hall, if you're nervous.'

'I'm not nervous with you here,' she said gratefully. 'That's if you're not *too* far away. I've never felt unsafe on Daramba before.'

Her tension was infectious. He felt a vague unease himself. Not that any trespasser on Daramba, let alone the homestead, wouldn't quickly see the error of his ways. The weapons in the gun room were kept under lock and key, but he knew where the key was and he was a crack shot. In a world gone mad, with violence escalating at a frightening rate, he'd had to confront the spectre of kidnap himself. It was always a possibility, but he thanked God he lived in a country where such things didn't happen. No one attacked giants of industry. His grandfather and Sir Francis had walked everywhere free as air. Their womenfolk and their offspring had also taken their safety completely for granted. But times had changed.

They were walking up the staircase together when Francesca, oddly off balance, surprised him with a question. 'Why did you tell Carina we were coming here this weekend?'

On edge himself, his answer was short and clipped. 'You're priceless—really.'

'What does that mean?'

'I've no time for all this nonsense about Carina.'

They had reached the gallery and he moved along it swiftly, a panther without its leash, so she had to increase her pace. He wanted to reach out for her. Hold her. His desire for her was pouring off him. Yet she chose to speak about Carina when all he wanted was to brush all thoughts of Carina aside.

'Well?' She caught his arm, feeling a stab of panic at the glitter in his eyes.

He swung about. 'What is it you want me to say?'

'God knows!' She dropped her hand, feeling confused and suddenly terribly lonely. 'I was a little hurt, that's all.'

'You mean you continue to believe *everything* she tells you?' He knew he was getting angrier by the moment, but for once he couldn't seem to get control. He moved off again, opening the door of the bedroom opposite hers. Unlike the one he usually occupied on his visits it wasn't made up, but who the hell cared? He wouldn't be getting any sleep.

'Don't be like this, Bryn,' she pleaded, coming to stand, shimmering, within the frame of the door, tormenting him. Water nymphs didn't have a heart. Yet hadn't he taken her small breast in his hand? Felt the heart beat?

'Ah, give me a break!' he responded. 'Are we *ever* going to be free of bloody Carina? She's fed you so much misinformation and downright lies since you were a child you don't seem able to see through her.'

'Are you saying you *didn't* tell her?'

'I'm not saying anything,' he said. 'If I can't get through to you by now I ought to give up trying.'

She moved a little further into the room. 'Okay, then, she was lying. She said you made the first move. You rang her. It was then you told her we were coming here for the weekend.'

'There you go! It must be true.' If she came any nearer he really would lose it.

She paused at the brilliant glitter in his eyes. 'Bryn… please, Bryn…'

'Don't you *dare* cry. Don't *do* this!'

His eyes blazed at her. Her tears goaded him.

'I'm sorry,' she said. 'I'm a fool. Carrie gets so many hooks into me they not only pierce my skin they drag me down. You must hate me at times.'

'Oh, yes—*hate!*' He was so wound up his tone could have stripped the skin from her. But the pressure inside him was building at a tremendous rate. A part of his brain told him not to frighten her—his job was to protect her, not to take what she couldn't give—but her beauty was all around him, scenting the very air. It stripped him of all resistance.

He thought she began a little glide towards him. Surely she did? He was almost gone.

'Francey!' he groaned. 'Lord, girl, don't you know how much I want you? I can't keep this up any more.'

He couldn't look like that, speak like that, unless he meant it. There was an *ache* in his voice; the worst kind of pain. He was begging her to be true to herself. She extended her slender arm so her fingertips, light and soft as silk, were just brushing his face.

They burned him like a brand. He tensed, every rippling muscle in his body knotting.

'I was betrayed, Bryn,' she whispered. 'You were betrayed…I—'

Frantic now, feeling the throbbing hardness in his body, he pulled her forcibly to him, his head swimming with sexual excitement and his need so intense he turned her in an instant to being utterly pliant in his arms. 'Don't…don't talk, Francey. I can't wait for you any longer.'

Her heart banged against her ribs. He was so strong she felt physically helpless, yet her instinct told her he would never hurt her. 'Then *don't* wait!' she cried. She was able to bring up her hands, locking them around his neck, her hips consciously working themselves against his highly aroused body. 'I can't wait either.' She put everything she felt for him into her emotion-charged admission.

Briefly she had a glimpse of the change that came over him. The anger disappeared, to be replaced by male exultation in all its forms. His physical power, considerable at any time, had increased. Much taller than she, now he seemed to *tower* over her, A fierce not-to-be-denied hunger glowed out of his dark, glittering eyes.

Holding her beautiful mouth with his, Bryn lifted her in one smooth, effortless movement, as though her slender body was weightless, and carried her across the hallway to her bedroom opposite…

CHAPTER SEVEN

JUST on a week later, they all sat in Francesca's office in serious discussion. Francesca had abandoned her position behind her grandfather's massive desk in favour of a comfortable armchair between Elizabeth and Annette.

'Ah—here's coffee!' she said a little time later, looking towards the door.

Valerie Scott, having tapped on the door, now came in, pushing a trolley bearing a silver tray set with a sterling silver coffee service and the finest English bone china. The wonderful aroma was of coffee freshly made, not from any machine. That would have been out of the question. A three-tiered cakestand held delicate sandwiches and a selection of cup cakes, beautifully decorated.

Francesca held up a hand, smiling at the woman who was proving an unobtrusive but very efficient staff member. 'Thank you, Valerie. This looks lovely.'

'I hope you enjoy it.' Valerie returned the smile, which embraced the two very elegant seated ladies, both of whom she knew—as she knew all the families. Mrs Elizabeth Forsyth and Mrs Annette Macallan. If privately she was wondering what they were doing here, she gave not the slightest sign. Valerie knew the late Sir Francis had taken Elizabeth Forsyth's departure from the family very badly indeed. She knew Elizabeth had not been a beneficiary of Sir Francis's will. She also knew the Macallan women loathed her late ex-lover. So here they were all together, Francesca, Annette and Elizabeth, obviously in perfect harmony.

Or they thought they were. Valerie Scott withdrew quietly, shutting the door.

'I'm a bit surprised you've kept her on, Francey,' Elizabeth said after a moment, a vaguely worried frown between her brows. 'You know she was—'

'Yes.' Francesca headed Elizabeth off. 'Actually, it's working out quite well. She's efficient, and very discreet.'

'Really?' Elizabeth raised her eyebrows, a droll expression on her face. 'She didn't exactly keep a low profile with my dear father-in-law.'

Annette swallowed a laugh.

'She's on her own, Elizabeth,' Francesca explained. 'No husband to support her. I didn't have the heart to move her on.'

'God forbid she'd be left to sell real estate, like another ex-member of Frank's club,' Elizabeth said.

'Not Sally McGuiness?' Annette stared at her friend in mild shock.

'So I've been told,' Elizabeth answered breezily. 'But Sally is a happy-go-lucky kind of girl. She'll be okay.'

'Grandfather didn't leave either of them a razoo, for all their grand affairs,' Fra.ncesca said, thinking that wasn't quite fair.

'The word is he gave Valerie more than enough when he was alive,' Elizabeth, the irrepressible, revealed. 'Anyway, let's forget Valerie. But I wouldn't trust her with too much, Francey,' she warned. 'Remember she *was* sleeping with the enemy.'

'Name me someone he *didn't* sleep with,' Annette broke in, uncharacteristically waspish. She rose to her smartly shod feet, a beautiful woman, dark-haired, dark-eyed, still retaining her girlish figure even though she had taken a back seat in life. 'I'll be mother.' She started to pour the coffee. 'Have you spoken to anyone else about this, Francey? Outside of Bryn, that is?'

'No one,' Francesca confirmed. 'I take it neither of you are opposed to the idea? I do so want you aboard.'

'I'm in,' Elizabeth cried in jolly fashion, accepting her exquisite cup and saucer from her lifelong friend. 'Thanks, dear. I'll enjoy it. It's rather thrilling being a defector. A bit like Nureyev. You're not going to let us down are you, Annie?'

Annette suddenly looked nervous, sinking her teeth in her bottom lip. 'I don't know if I could pull my weight.' Carefully she placed a sandwich and a cup cake on each plate. 'I would hate to let you down, Francey. I've been so out of everything. Rather like a woman in a coma.'

'Time now to break out of it, love,' Elizabeth told her friend firmly. 'You're highly intelligent and you're utterly trustworthy. Francey needs people like us around her. That's why she's asked. It saddens me to say it, but you can bet your life my daughter, who doesn't wish to have anything to do with me, would like nothing better than to see Francey come a cropper. Not that it's likely to happen. I've had my ear to the ground, Francey, and the word is you're turning out trumps. Lady

Macallan is still a real powerhouse. She can handle the Macallan side of things on her own. Francey and I need you here, Annie. Don't we, Francey?'

'It would make me feel so much more secure.' Francesca turned to Annette with an encouraging smile. 'The whole place is regularly swept for bugs—courtesy of the age we live in—but I still don't have a clue how Carrie found out Bryn and I were flying to Daramba last weekend. *She* told me it was Bryn.'

'She wanted to upset and confuse you,' Annette said, her expression showing a flicker of anger. 'I don't like to speak ill of anyone—' Annette reached out to pat Elizabeth's hand tenderly '—but if I were you, Francey, I'd take everything Carrie says from now on, especially in relation to Bryn, with a pinch of salt. We all know how she feels about him.'

Elizabeth sighed deeply. 'My daughter has never in her life been thwarted. Her grandfather and her father spoilt her terribly. Both of them rode roughshod over me. Charles has actually admitted it.'

'Really?' Annette asked quickly, rounding on her friend.

'A whole new Charles has emerged since his father died,' Elizabeth told them, going a little pink. 'I think he's trying to get back with me.'

'Are you going to let him?' Annette didn't look at all happy about that eventuality.

'We'll see!' Mischief shimmered out of Elizabeth's fine grey eyes. 'Charles was a different man in the early years, you know. It was later, after we lost Lionel when he began to turn into a control freak like Frank. Simply copied him. Though it *was* the way to go. The only one exempt was Carrie, who really needed a firm hand. Free of his father's dominance, and with Bryn taking over the reins at Titan, Charles isn't under tremendous stress every second. He's much better suited to being supportive.'

'Well, he has a way to go before he'll win *me* over, Liz,' Annette said with asperity. 'They gave you a bad time.'

'I know. I know. But it will never happen again!' Elizabeth stoutly raised her coffee cup. 'Of that you can be sure.' She took a long, appreciative sip. 'This coffee is very good. But for now, Annie, we've got to concentrate on helping Francey out. What d'you think?' She spoke briskly, having lived a long time with her friend's reluctance to participate in most endeavours. 'We need an answer, my girl. That means *today!*'

Annette buried her small nose in her own coffee cup. Then slowly she raised her head, her flashing smile lifting ten years off her. 'If you *really* want me, the answer is yes!'

'Let's get Valerie back in with a bottle of champagne,' Elizabeth suggested, full of cheer. She'd had serious reservations about Annette committing when Francesca had first spoken to her of her intentions. They both knew Annette had been letting the days of her life drift away, with time running out. It was enormously heartening to see that beautiful, flashing smile that her son had inherited along with her midnight-dark eyes. With any luck at all, Annette was back!

It was enough to move those who loved her to tears.

Francesca lost no time contacting the highly regarded landscape designer Gordon Carstairs. Lady Macallan had suggested him, and had probably swung the deal as she'd spoken to the designer directly. Carstairs had extensive experience, having worked on large estates in the United Kingdom as well as France, Italy, Austria and

Greece. His home bases were London and Sydney. He had just returned from creating from scratch a very large private garden in Sri Lanka, so Francesca was able to approach him at a period when he was blessedly free. At least for a time.

They met several times, over lunch and at the office. Carstairs, in his mid-fifties, was a fine-looking man with a striking head of pewter-grey hair. A six footer, he was very lean and strong, with great ease and a charm of manner which must have worked well with his international clients. He and Francesca got on extremely well, having similar tastes. They soon decided on a date to fly out to Daramba, so Gordon could make a detailed study of the site which, as Francesca had explained to him was 'relatively leafless'. The date was set for the end of the month, which gave them ten days.

Francesca was right in the thick of foundation business, but she quickly found her job was made easier by having Elizabeth and Annette on board. The two women, close friends and on the same wavelength, consequently worked very well together, sometimes in tandem, depending on circumstance. Best of all, they shared a fierce commitment to Francey and an intense dedication—qualities that worked extremely well for Francey *and* the Forsyth Foundation. At the end of the day Elizabeth and Annette, being who they were, knew everyone who was anyone, and everyone knew them.

The big surprise was Annette. She had taken no time at all to break out of her shell. Once she had even joined Francesca and Gordon over lunch, blossoming in their company and asking Gordon a good many pertinent questions. She had been far more animated than Francesca had ever seen her. Indeed, although Francesca had made no comment to anyone, including Bryn, it seemed to her that Annette and Gordon had not only clicked, they had been instantly attracted to each other.

Annette had mourned her late husband for many years. Without a word being spoken, society had accepted that Annette Macallan would never remarry. No one could take her husband's place. No one had the temerity to try. It was as though she had died with him. All over! Such a waste! Her meeting with Gordon Carstairs had opened up a whole new frontier. Gordon was free. An early marriage had failed—with no children—although he told them he was still good friends with his ex-wife, who had since remarried.

Much, much too early to say, but Francesca had her hopes. Life flowed on like a river. Time now for Annette to be happy again.

Early evening, when the deep blue sky was lightening to mauve, Bryn let himself in to Francesca's apartment. He had his own key. Although he spoke to her on a daily basis, and again last thing at night, it wasn't enough since their weekend at Daramba.

As Titan's new CEO—it had caused scarcely a ripple on the stock market and in the business world—he had begun initiating many changes, holding meeting after meeting. Not all of them had gone smoothly. But he had fully expected that. He was still explaining to the new people he had put in place precisely what he wanted. It was a hands-on affair, an all out effort, so he could be sure his new policies would not only be thoroughly understood, but implemented a.s.a.p. There never seemed to be enough time.

He was also part—'an important part', as the Premier of the State had stressed—of a trade delegation leaving for China in two days' time. China was their major trading partner. He only wished that like his country's Prime Minister he was fluent in Mandarin.

He had a romantic evening planned. A very special night! They weren't going out to dinner. Both of them wanted to stay at home. Francey had assured him she was already stocked up. Not that he cared so much about dinner. It was Francey he was hungry for. Every minute they spent with each other was precious. They didn't want anyone else around.

He put his attaché case down, shrugged out of his jacket, then walked to the drinks trolley, thinking he would have a Scotch on the rocks while he was waiting. Francey had promised him she would be home by seven. He couldn't wait to see her. Her beauty, her intelligence, her emotional capacity overwhelmed him. It was the sweetest, sweetest pain just thinking about her when they were apart.

High time they were at the very least engaged. Maybe six months on they could set a wedding date. He loved her to the point where he couldn't do without her. He wanted her always *there*, at his side. He and Francesca made quite a pair. He and his grandmother were enormously grateful to her for the way she had coaxed his mother onto her team. It had been a huge coup. He hadn't seen his mother so whole heartedly involved in life since before his father had died. Not only had she become entirely 'with it', she had updated every aspect of her appearance. Always beautiful and quietly elegant, her new and more youthful image was drawing a lot of positive attention.

'Annette has come back to us!' his grandmother had said. 'And who do we thank but our little Francey?'

Francesca took a phone call from Carina a bare ten minutes before she wanted to leave the building. It had come as a puzzlement to her, the way Carina had turned virtually overnight into the sort of cousin she had always wanted. They had only met up once or twice since their grandfather's death, and then only for coffee—Francesca had too many demands on her time—but Carina had dropped her hard brilliance in favour of a much softer, more affectionate approach. She rang at least once a week—'just keeping in touch!'—even going so far as to say she was okay with the fact her mother and Annette Macallan were now working for the Forsyth Foundation.

'A little bird tells me Annette has taken a shine

to the landscaper Gordon Carstairs,' she announced now, as though imparting a secret pleasing to them both. 'That's lovely. I know how much Annette adored her husband, but let's face it, life goes on. She's still only young. What? Fifty? She deserves some happiness.'

She did indeed, thought Francesca, but there was something not *right* about Carrie's saying it. Carrie had been quite scathing about Annette and her withdrawal from life in the past. 'It's hardly gone as far as that, Carrie,' she answered, brushing Gordon aside. But all in a good cause. 'You're remarkably well informed.'

Carina gave a laugh as sharp as a piece of broken glass. 'For goodness' sake, Francey, everyone knows Mum and Annette are working for you. As for Carstairs—who, incidentally, is quite a hunk for his age—friends of mine were seated at a table not far from the three of you in a restaurant.'

'What restaurant?'

'Gosh, I dunno. One of the top. It's hard to keep secrets, pet. Everyone knows what's going on. What I particularly wanted to ask you is, when next you go to Daramba could I please come too? I'd love to meet Gordon. I've been thinking we need a really first-class landscaper at the house.

Dad doesn't care what changes I make. I suppose you know he's trying to win Mum back?'

Francesca swallowed. Carrie at Daramba? 'And how do you feel about that—seeing *you* haven't contacted your mother?' She played for time.

Carina's soft chuckle came over the wires. 'You know I want to. But, look—it ain't easy. As for Mum and Dad getting back together again—I'd be *thrilled*.'

'Nice if you'd ring and tell her that,' Francesca said. 'As for their getting back together, that's up to Liz.'

'Absolutely!' Carina confirmed. 'Now, about Daramba?'

Francesca sat back in her chair, half horrified by the request. 'Carrie, I don't—'

'Please!' her cousin interrupted. 'I don't ask for much. Besides, it will do us both good to spend time together.'

'I'll get back to you,' Francesca promised at last. 'But for now I must fly.'

'Bye-bye, then,' Carina carolled breezily. 'It must be time for you to walk out the door. You know what they say. All work and no play... Dinner at home with Bryn this evening?'

It was very difficult to get a handle on this new

and yet familiar Carina. How did she know so much? Or was she simply fishing? On the other hand, it could all be true. Carina had simply turned into a better person. 'No plans as yet, Carrie.'

'Give him my love. And wish him a safe trip from me. Bryn is a wonderful ambassador for this country,' she said warmly, with no trace whatsoever of lingering bitter resentment. 'No wonder you look to him for everything.' There was a pregnant pause, as if Carina was expecting a prompt response. None was forthcoming. 'Lovely to talk to you, Francey,' she said into the void. 'And thanks for everything. For being so understanding. I know my behaviour has caused you a lot of grief. But that's all over now. First cousins are meant by the very nature of things to be close. Don't forget, now. Give me a ring. I feel so much better about our relationship these days, don't you?'

Francesca tried desperately to inject an answering warmth into her voice. 'I always wanted us to be the best of friends, Carrie,' she said. Lord knew it was true. But what would it take? She had glimpsed their grandfather in Carrie once too often. These present overtures could be nothing more than Carina's sugar-coated controlling mechanisms. Uncertain in her judgement, Francesca eased back. Surely Carina deserved a second chance? 'Bye, now, Carrie,' she said gently. 'Take care.'

Carefully she put the receiver down, breaking the connection. The truth was—and she couldn't suppress it—she didn't want Carina on Daramba. Especially not when Annette and Gordon were there. She wanted harmony, not trouble. She knew both Annette and Carina's own mother, Elizabeth, were convinced Carina was merely playing games.

'Happy families!' Elizabeth had remarked, with considerable irony.

It was something of a dilemma. If Carina really had undergone a miraculous sea change wouldn't she be bitterly insulted, perhaps irrevocably, if she were denied an invitation to Daramba? After all it was the flagship of the Forsyth pastoral empire, and Carina was very much a Forsyth. It was quite possible Carina genuinely intended to bring a top-class landscaper in, to create a more beautiful and softening environment for the Forsyth mausoleum.

If she said yes to Carina there could be no going back on it. Saying no would be the truly difficult part. She and Carina were of the same blood.

Only blood had been let.

* * *

She was no sooner in the door, calling jubilantly, 'I'm home!' when Bryn appeared—so vivid, so remarkable. In his presence her energies were re-charged.

'It's marvellous to see you!'

She laughed. 'How long has it been since I've seen you?'

'Getting on for fifty-eight hours too long,' he replied, drawing her with an electrifying desire into his arms. 'And, God, how I've missed you! Every second of the day, and worse at night!' Black eyes tender but turbulent, he thrust his strong hand into her lustrous hair as he positioned her face at exactly the right angle for his passion-ate, welcoming kiss.

Predictably, it turned into kiss...after kiss... after kiss...

Delicate, tantalising little nips and nuzzles, starving little exhalations, in between open-mouthed expressions of the deepest desire, rapidly passing to a tension that built so merci-lessly high that kissing was nowhere near enough. They wanted to go to bed. Each was bent on seeking the ultimate physical contact, yearning bodies fused, limbs entwined. Consummation was sublime—especially when they had been deprived of each other for even a short time.

'I understand that,' she whispered.

Neither of them spoke again as he began removing her structured black jacket with its nipped-in waist, turning away briefly to place it over the back of one of the antique Regency chairs that stood on either side of the console. That done, he began slowly unbuttoning her silk blouse. The front was ruched, the colour an exquisite teal-blue. Francesca's every last barricade was long since demolished. Bryn had held up a mirror to her own beauty; to its softness, voluptuousness and, for him, its utter desirability. When they made love, which was every time they came together, they did so with a flawless intensity—as if each was desperate to find out what lay behind the flesh of the other. It was truly as though they both sought to be *one.*

He broke off nuzzling the swan curve of her neck. 'Dinner can wait?'

She thought she murmured, 'Yes!' But she couldn't be sure, her emotions were so extravagantly unbridled.

'I'll take that as a yes.' He laughed deep in his throat, a man at peace, but his hands on her were urgent.

Finally she stood naked, as slender as a water reed, her feverish blood colouring her olive skin pink.

'At last we're alone!' he groaned. 'The more I get of you, the more I want!'

'It's the same with me.' The profound truth.

'Wonderful!' He hugged her warm body to him, his hand pressed against the smooth curve of her lower back. 'Communion like we have, Francey, comes rarely.'

A stab of fear touched her heart. 'Bryn, no—hush!' She stopped him by placing a warning finger against his lips. 'Is it possible to love too much? It could attract the attention of jealous gods.' That flicker of fear—the fear of loss—showed in her beautiful eyes.

'Then we have to draw a magic circle around us,' he answered, wrapping his arms fiercely around her. 'When you go to Daramba at the weekend speak to Jili. She's right up there with the magic potions and spells. Whatever the past, Francey, and our personal tragedies, we have to leave them behind and face the future with confidence. From now on I'll always be by your side.'

Dinner had been forgotten. They lay quietly in bed, in thrall with one another, only the faint echoes of their impassioned moans left inside the room. All energy was spent, so overwhelming had been their lovemaking. Bryn lay on his back, one arm behind his dark head, and Francesca spooned into him, her heartbeat striking into his side, one arm flung across his naked chest, one foot hooked around his ankle.

'You're the most wonderful lover in the entire universe!' she gasped, her fingers working the hair on his chest into tiny curls. 'That was ravishing!'

'*You're* ravishing,' he replied, dropping a kiss on the top of her head. Conversation was out of the question. They were still floating in the aftermath of sexual bliss. After a few more minutes of drifting, Bryn suddenly said, 'By the way, I've got something for you.'

'You've always got something for me.' She smiled. Flowers, jewellery, a beautiful piece of Chinese porcelain to add to her collection…

'You haven't asked what it is.' He slid out of the tangle of sheets, a living sculpture, his naked body lightly sheened with sweat, little scratches from her long nails showing faintly red against the gilded bronze of his flesh. She had never in her life scratched a man before Bryn.

'Show me,' she invited, luxuriously stretching her legs and curling her toes. With the way they made love, she had inevitably began thinking about the children they would have in, say, a year or so. The power they had to make new life she found sacred. So tragically deprived of her parents, and at such an early age, she had the most intense desire to have a family of her own. Bryn's child, her child—their kids. Beautiful children, to reinforce their great love. Her path in life that had once been littered with pain and confusion was now clear. No more dead ends. No more dark alleys. Home was Bryn.

He was saying something. What?

'I have every intention of showing you. First I'll find my robe. I need to look my best.'

'You look your best now!' Her laugh rippled. She was in awe of his superb physique. 'Your robe is behind the bathroom door, where you left it.' She pushed another pillow behind her head. What was it this time? It didn't matter. It could be a cone shell off the beach. She would still love it.

He was back within a minute, wearing the dark red robe that made such a splash of colour against his darkly tanned skin, and carrying a tiny box in his hand.

She sat up quickly, saying tremulously, 'Bryn?'

'You never suspected?'

'No.'

'I don't believe you.' He sat down on the bed beside her.

'It's true.' She felt such a rush of excitement it was hard to stop her voice trembling.

'You *are* going to marry me?' His dark eyes swept her lovely face, seeing her sudden agitation.

'Oh, yes—*yes,* please.' She articulated it as though reciting a vow. 'I adore you.'

'Then we have to get engaged first—don't you agree?' he asked quietly.

'Oh, Bryn!' She tossed her long hair, damp at the temples, from her face, so it cascaded down her bare back. Just as she was thinking herself strong and secure she experienced a tiny frisson of fear about the timing. She had endured too many years of Carina's conditioning to throw off her cousin's influence overnight. Despite Carina's apparent coming to terms with their new lives and status, she felt thoroughly unnerved by the prospect that Carina mightn't be able to handle the fact of an engagement between her and Bryn so soon! Not that Bryn wouldn't be there for her—her rock in life.

'I thought we were going to wait a while?'

'Unacceptable. I live and breathe *you.*'

Such knowledge was thrilling, yet it scared her

a little. Certain people were destined for loss. One saw it all the time.

Bryn touched a finger to the beating pulse in her throat. 'You're too tender-hearted for you own good, Francey. You're thinking of how Carina will react?'

She looked away. She couldn't hide a thing from him. He knew her too well.

'No, look at me,' Bryn said, and made sure of it by placing his hand firmly around her chin. 'You feel sorry for her?'

'Of course I do.' Her iridescent eyes pleaded with him for understanding. 'She *is* my cousin. She's been reared to believe in her divine right to have everything she wants.'

'And you're convinced she wants *me?*' He gave a slight and dangerous smile.

'You know she does. When it comes to you she's a bit deranged. All this current stuff, the way she goes on, is false. At least I *think* it's false.'

'Francey, you have to make up your mind. While Carrie has been supposedly so hotly desirous of me she's been living a downright promiscuous life. And she's been quite vocal about it.'

'Just distractions!' Francesca wrote her cousin's multiple short lived affairs off. 'Trying to make you jealous. I don't know. Who knows Carrie? Not even her mother.' Colour swept into her cheeks. 'I love you, Bryn. God knows, I love you. I want to announce our engagement too.'

'You think this is a *ring*?'

'Isn't it?' Her eyes went wide.

'Of course it is!' He dropped a chastening kiss on her mouth. 'Why don't you have a look?'

'You're angry with me,' she said.

'Not yet.' But his look was very direct. 'Open the box, Francey. I love you. I've always loved you. I want to spend the rest of my life with you. I want you to be the mother of our children. But I'm damned if I'm going to let Carina into our magic circle. If she could, Carina would deny you any chance at happiness. She has wanted nothing more than that since she was a child. Not even me. Surely to God you've come to that realisation?'

'Yes, I have. But it's still a bit new. She's so clever. I was starting to think maybe she really *wanted* us to be friends.'

'Then you'd better think again,' Bryn said, his voice bone-dry.

'All I want to think of is you and me.'

'That's my girl!' he said with open exultation.

Her heart contracted at the sight of the diamond engagement ring that sat so proudly inside the silk-lined box. It was glorious! A great ring for a great occasion! The glittering central stone was a flawless white, its brilliance offset by a garland of precious Arygle pink diamonds from their own Western Australia mines in the fabled Kimberley region. Argyle was the world's major source of rare pink diamonds, and this ring's masterly designer had used them to the utmost effect.

'Well?' he asked tenderly, sympathetic to the pile-up of emotions that had to some extent wounded her psyche.

She stared into his dynamic face, half in shadow, half in gilded light. 'I couldn't have wished for a more perfect ring. I love it. I love *you!*'

'I was aware of that, my darling,' he said gently. 'But hang on!' Swiftly, he rose. 'This calls for a toast. This calls for champagne.'

'It does.' She went to get out of bed to join him.

'No, stay there.' He held up a hand. 'I want you in bed. I'll be back in a moment.'

He returned with a bottle of champagne and two crystal flutes. He put the flutes down gently, then grasped the base of the bottle with one hand, the other stripping away the foil. 'Now, this is a trick of mine, Francey. Watch carefully. I won't lose a drop.' With his thumb he dislodged the cork and it flew away, landing safely on the carpet.

'Bravo!' She clapped her hands. 'I'm impressed.'

'I have other skills.'

'I *know!*' She blushed deeply all over her body.

They sipped their champagne slowly, observing one another with elated and loving eyes. Bryn had already slipped the ring down over her slender finger, where it sat perfectly.

'It may be that you don't want to wear your ring openly until I get back from China,' he said, correctly gauging her transparent expression. 'I understand you want me with you when we announce our engagement.'

'I do.'

'Okay.' He lifted her hand and kissed it, turning it to press his mouth to the inner tracery of blue veins. 'Let it dwell between your breasts,' he said, and bent to kiss that scented spot. 'But when I get back we make the announcement—agreed?'

'Yes,' she breathed softly, holding up her left hand to the light. 'This is something I could only dream about.'

'No dream, my darling.' His sense of purpose

and determination showed itself in his voice and the glitter of his eyes. 'Drink up,' he urged. 'I want to make love to you all over again.'

CHAPTER EIGHT

SHE hadn't for a moment expected Annette to want to join the hunt for the killer dingo. Annette was a good rider, but hunting down rogue animals wasn't her thing. For one thing she had never fired a gun in her life, though she had been a guest on great Outback cattle stations many times in her life. No, Annette shied away from any form of violence, especially blood and killing, but violence was being done to Daramba's precious calves, too weak to save themselves, or to old and helpless animals that roamed the desert fringe.

Bloodthirsty dingoes struck terror. The most vicious and powerful had been known to attack a lone man. Daramba's men had by now taken to calling the dingo crossbreed The Ripper, because of the powerful animal's peculiarly brutal manner of ripping open the flesh of all the unfortunate calves it had stalked and brought down. It wasn't simply hunger, the need to sustain itself, the brute had developed a taste for blood.

The new man, Vance Bormann, out rounding up clean skins in the lignum thickets over the past few days, had sighted the dingo away from the pack. He had taken a shot at it—and he hated to admit it but The Ripper had got away, bounding off into the farther reaches of the lignum swamp. At least it gave them a clue as to where the dingo pack was currently hiding out. Bormann had told them he had found, to his disgust, the carcass of a newborn calf at the scene and buried it.

So the hunt was on. Gordon Carstairs very much wanted to be part of it. He told them quite matter-of-factly he was a good shot and an experienced rider. He'd grown up on a Victorian country estate, and although he hadn't been asked to prove it, after ten minutes with Jacob, who was now Daramba's overseer, Jacob had come back to Francesca with: 'He's a damned fine shot, Ms Francey. It'll be good to have 'im along.'

Annette, it seemed, had got caught up in the excitement. Or perhaps more accurately caught up in the excitement of Gordon Carstairs. Francesca was certain Annette had never expected to find love again—indeed she had turned her back on it—but the strong attraction between the two was plain to see. So Annette wanted to come along, but she would ride to the rear, ready if necessary to box the dingo in. That was if they were lucky enough to sight it or the pack.

'What the hell does Annette think she's doing, riding along?' Carina asked Francesca, angry bafflement on her face. She paused for a moment, as though seeking a solution to a serious problem. 'By far the most sensible thing for her to be doing is staying here at the homestead. You should insist. She'll only be a liability.'

Francesca couldn't really argue with that, but she hadn't had the heart to refuse Annette any more than she had found the heart to exclude Carina from this trip. So far everything had gone well, with Carina as charming and accommodating as Francesca had ever seen her. Now she had to intervene. 'Please don't say that to her, Carrie. Annette is the happiest I've ever seen her. I'm not going to allow anyone to spoil that. You've been so nice to her up to date. Don't spoil it now.'

'Sure!' Carina appeared to shrug her bafflement off. 'It's Gordon, of course!' She gave a knowing laugh. 'He's an old-fashioned man in his way—very gentlemanly and so forth. Annette would like that.'

'I like it too,' Francesca said. Were good manners old-fashioned? She thought not.

'Well, you and Annette aren't dissimilar in type,' Carina said, giving her cousin a considering once-over. 'You know—super-refined. I expect that's why Bryn decided you were more suitable than me. I'm too *out there*. It wouldn't have worked with Bryn and me anyway. I suppose that's why I've found it so easy to move on.' She went to press a real kiss onto Francesca's cheek. The first one Francesca had ever received. 'The great thing is that we're talking, Francey. We're friends again. If Carstairs is in favour with poor Annette, then he's in favour with me.'

Half the hunt got away early: Jacob, Carina—who could ride and shoot with the best of them—Vince Bormann, and two of the station's leading hands. Francesca, Gordon, Annette and three aboriginal stockmen-trackers followed. The sun was up and the mirage was already abroad. Francesca made sure Annette's fine skin was protected, swapping her own best cream Akubra with the ornate snake-skin band for Annette's less effective wide-brimmed black hat, and tucking a favourite sapphire-blue and white bandana into the neckline of Annette's long-sleeved cotton shirt to protect her nape. She wore the full-length sleeves for extra protection, but it wasn't long before Francesca saw her turning the cuffs up to the elbow. All in all, Annette looked immensely stylish. As slender as when she'd been a girl in her riding gear—especially the tight-fitting jeans, which looked great on her. Francesca could see Gordon thought so too.

Mid-morning and The Ripper hadn't been sighted—although the party had flushed out a few dingoes, their yellow-brown coats merging with the colour and texture of the scorched grasses. Spotted, they'd made a run for the hill country, moving at top speed, their desert-lean bodies flattened out with the effort. Jacob had waved a hand, which meant let them go. No love was lost on dingoes, but it was The Ripper they were after. They were to concentrate all their energies on that.

They were all strung out over a broad area of hundreds of yards. Francesca and Annette were away to the rear, with Francesca keeping her eye on the older woman. The horses were tiring. Morale was running low.

'What the hell?' Carina was way ahead, with one

of the stockmen. When she shouted, her voice carried a long distance on the clear air. She threw up a hand, gesturing towards a dried-up water course with a heavy surround of trees.

What was she shouting for? Francesca had to ask herself. If Carina *had* spotted The Ripper she would only alert the cunning animal. A glance passed between her and Annette. 'Do you want to go back now, Annette?' Francesca asked. 'You could take shelter under the trees.'

'I just might!' Annette said, a look of relief coming over her face.

'It's very tiring,' Francesca said quietly. 'I'm starting to feel a little shaky myself. My muscles haven't had such a workout in ages.'

Annette nodded, then turned her horse's head in the direction of the nearest billabong. 'Are you going on?'

'Just for a while,' Francesca said. 'Stay in the vicinity. We'll come back for you.'

'I'm fine, Francey. Don't worry. I know where I am,' Annette told her with a reassuring smile. 'Good luck now.'

For some reason Francesca didn't take the route the rest of them had taken. She had the feeling she was being led, that her route was charged with more purpose than finding the rogue dingo. She was *meant* to come this way. For most of her life she had had these mysterious intuitions. She wondered if other people did. Surely they must?

Riding deep in under the trees, she saw to her left a waterhole, glittering like a shallow lake, though she knew from experience it would be deep enough at the centre. Something splashed close in to the reed banks. She froze.

Nothing, though her skin was prickling. Gamely she rode on, her face and her neck streaked with sweat, rivulets running between her breasts. The air was getting thicker and danker. Her nerves were crawling. The deeper in she went, the more she thought she could smell dingo. The others were coming back now. Unsuccessful. She could hear raised voices, the thunder of hooves. She even caught Jacob's dejected yell.

'The bastard ain't here, or he got away!'

Her shoulders rode high and tight. She was very nervous. So was Jalilah. Just a few hundred yards on, the dark green undergrowth became thicker, darker and more tangled, making it difficult for her to proceed or continue searching for tracks. But the smell of dingo *filled* her nostrils. Dread began a slow crawl over her skin. This, then, was where their quarry was waiting. She knew it. She had succumbed to the compulsion. Now alone, she was riding right at The Ripper.

It was enormous for a pure-bred dingo. It was difficult to say who took the most fright. The dingo, in a lather of sweat so its matted coat looked a mangy, orange-streaked grey, slunk back, crouching down on its haunches. No use trying to keep it off by shouting or clapping. She could see that wouldn't work. The dingo was intent on her. Teeth bared, it looked at her with what seemed like human hatred, though that had to be her over-active imagination. Nevertheless it made the short hairs stand up on the back of her neck.

The animal began to snarl, its ferocity and sheer size bringing on a moment of sheer panic. She had seen dingoes all her life, but nothing like this. This wasn't the average wild dog. This was a monster. It wasn't going to retreat. But Francesca's nerves had begun to attack, and the mare, spooked by the presence of the dingo, was acting up. Dingo or not, it looked more like a lion ready to spring.

It couldn't reach her upper body—or could it?—but it could savage her foot, or Jalilah's legs and sides. She heard shots. Marvelled at them. One seemed very close. Too close. She hadn't expected that one. Her hands that one moment had been shaky now steadied on the .22 rifle. She had a job to do. This was *her* world, and this was one dingo who had to go.

'All right—come on!' Francesca muttered at the beast, in the process passing on courage to herself. 'Come *on!*'

The dingo needed no further urging. It leapt for her, as though she were no more than its next victim to be ripped to shreds, but Francesca, ice-cool, got off a single shot.

The bullet sped to its mark, penetrating the rogue dingo's brain.

Hey, little one!

Near startled out of her wits, Francesca swung her head sharply. She didn't know the soft voice, but it was aboriginal. There was no one in sight, which her mind found unacceptable.

Hey, little one, can you hear me?

The voice came again. From where? The water-hole? The reeds were flattened over a wide area. The dingo had most probably torn through the area, snapping them off. It seemed to her for a trance-like moment that the grasses were stained with blood. She blinked, by now dumbstruck, and when she opened her eyes again the bloodstains were gone. Incredible! Her body rocked a little in the saddle. The heat and the kill. It was proving too much for her.

'Who's there?' she called, trying to inject authority into her shaky voice. 'Show yourself.'

What did she expect? An aboriginal figure to slide out of the water and into her field of vision? The voice *was* aboriginal. No question. But now, to her further astonishment, the whole scene that had been bathed in a deep green gloom changed dramatically. The sun slanted through the high branches of the Red River gums, vividly illuminating the deep waterhole.

Francesca sat her horse, confounded, watching ripples fan out wide over the water. There was no wind. No movement in the air. The branches of the trees were still. She felt as if she was having an out of body experience, but curiously she was not alarmed. Someone, some entity, was trying to tell her something. Make her pay attention. A vivid imagination was part of her. She had to accept that. It worked supremely well for her as an artist, but sometimes it could work against her. She listened a little longer. Nothing. She tried to remember who had called her *little one*. The 'one' had been clearly articulated. Taree Newton had always called her *little 'un*. It wasn't Taree's voice. Aboriginal, but more city-educated. She would have been very glad to see him, but Taree hadn't come on the hunt. At his age, he wasn't up to it. A memory long-forgotten stirred, then as quickly faded out.

'I'll come back,' she promised, though she couldn't begin to explain why she said it, or to whom.

The mare delicately skirted the body of the dead dingo, hoofs high, returning almost of its own accord along the rough trail Francesca had blazed. It wasn't until she reached the open plain that she saw Carina, riding towards her as if a gang of cattle rustlers was hot on her trail. Her mount looked almost out of control, though Carina was an experienced rider. When she and Francesca met up, a hundred yards off, Francesca saw her cousin's face was streaming with tears. Carina was sobbing, struggling for breath. In an instant Francesca's heart went cold with fear. She had never in her life seen her cousin in such a state.

'There's been an accident,' Carina gasped, swiping the wetness from her face, her hand like a washcloth. 'Annette. She's been shot.'

'Dear God, no!' A fine trembling started up in Francesca, spreading from her chest into her stomach and limbs. Had Annette been brought down by the shots that had preceded her own? Sick to the point where bile was rising to her throat, Francesca kicked her mare into action. Unless she had shifted out of the designated area, Annette should have been perfectly safe.

Annette had been extremely lucky. The only reason she was still alive was at the last moment the man sent to terminate Francesca Forsyth's life had realised he was targeting the wrong woman. Abruptly he had changed aim, so that the bullet glanced off her arm, high up, near the shoulder. Fool that he was, he had mistaken Annette Macallan for his target. The woman was of a height, with the same very slender build, and she was wearing the cream Akubra and the blue bandana he had been alerted to look for. Even when she had turned her head she had momentarily confused him. She was a beautiful woman, but at the very least twenty or more years older than his target. There would be no pay-off for killing the wrong woman.

Swiftly Bormann had remounted, then ridden

like the wind. When the woman was found he would be nowhere near her. Some of the others had got off a few shots. Hadn't he and the Bitch been the ones to incite them? This whole thing was an accident. The woman could hardly say otherwise. She hadn't even been aware of him.

It was Bryn when he returned home—he had cut short his China trip—who hit on his own theory for the shooting 'accident'. It came to him the instant his mother mentioned in passing that she had been wearing Francesca's Akubra, and that Francesca had also lent her a blue bandana to protect the vulnerable skin of her nape. He took time to think it out. His mind searched for alternative explanations for the bizarre incident, but nothing carried the weight or the logic of his own scenario.

Francesca had been the target. Not his mother. Not that he could alarm Francesca by telling her that. What proof did he have, anyway?

His mother had started walking the length of the lagoon when she had heard shots being fired. There had been a lot of shouting as well. She had grown afraid. Everyone in the party had an alibi, if indeed an alibi was needed. He could be wrong. There were no witnesses to anything. Quite a few shots had been fired to flush out the animal. No one else believed for a moment it was anything but a near tragic accident. There was no reason in the world for anyone to want to hurt Mrs Macallan. She had been in the wrong place at the wrong time. The stray bullet had mercifully glanced off her shoulder. All the flowing blood had made the injury seem much worse than it actually was.

His mother was already on her way to a full recovery, with Gordon Carstairs dancing attendance, seemingly unable to get back to work. Annette would bear a scar, but nothing cosmetic surgery couldn't fix. Everyone on the station had been extremely upset. Carina had needed sedation, so severe had been her reaction. Francesca had astonished herself by taking charge. No police had been called in. It would have taken hours for them to get there in any case. Daramba had always looked after its own. A doctor well known to them had been flown in to attend to Annette.

Even so, Carina had been quite right. Annette should have stayed back at the homestead, where she would have been perfectly safe. Francesca felt she had to bear a lot of the blame, though Annette wouldn't hear a word of it.

'My own fault, Francey,' she said, gently holding Francesca's hand. 'You told me to stay put, not walk into the danger zone.'

Still her son was not convinced. And what the hell was that? Carina requiring sedation? Carina and his mother had never got on. More likely Carina was hiding from a plan gone wrong. Bryn thought back to how at the end his grandfather had come to believe his partner had got rid of Gulla Nolan. Frank Forsyth would have had his reasons. Gulla might have had something on him. It had been no accident at all. Carina had more than a dollop of her ruthless, unforgiving grandfather's blood. And she was an excellent markswoman. When she'd realised she had the wrong target in her sights, she'd veered off before making her getaway. No one was likely to suspect let alone question a Forsyth. A woman, moreover, so distressed she had to be sedated.

All the more reason to get Carina to admit it, Bryn thought. Francesca had to be protected at all costs.

It was Elizabeth who gave him the lever. She was the one to unmask the mole in their midst. She had gone to Valerie Scott to ask for the schedule for any upcoming meetings Francesca was to have with those seeking potential grants. She had, in fact, fully expected to have the schedule on her desk that morning. Not finding Valerie in her place, Elizabeth had decided the schedule was most probably in a drawer. When it was not easily sighted amid the paperwork, Elizabeth had pulled out an entire drawer to give it a thorough search. It was then she'd come upon what she'd at first thought was a state-of-the-art mobile phone. She had never come across one like it.

She was busy examining it, frowning in a troubled fashion, when Valerie returned from a visit to the restroom.

Elizabeth looked up and met the other woman's eyes. Immediately it struck Elizabeth like a bolt of lightning. Valerie Scott was their mole. It wasn't simply Valerie's violent flush that gave her away. Elizabeth had had her doubts about Mrs. Scott right from the beginning. Her loyalty could well have been given to her ex-lover's immediate family and not to Francesca, whom she must have thought of as a usurper. Elizabeth was certain that with this sophisticated gadget Valerie Scott would have been able to monitor all of Francesca's calls and pass on information. She might even have been able to relay the calls directly, for all Elizabeth knew. Right now it was a matter for security.

Elizabeth lost no time getting them up to the executive floor, motioning to the Scott woman—stricken now she was found out, and making no attempt to brazen it out—to sit down and await her fate.

'I can't believe it. I can't deal with it.' Bryn had just finished telling Francesca of his suspicions, and the reasons for them. 'Carrie couldn't want to *kill* me. She couldn't! That's a great sin.' Shock and revulsion were in Francesca's voice. 'Was she trying to frighten me off, do you think?'

'Frighten you off the planet,' Bryn retorted grimly, keeping his arms around her. 'I had Elizabeth ring her with a message from you saying you'd like her to come to the apartment this evening around seven, if she can make it. She told Liz she could.'

'But that's in twenty minutes.' Francesca's head shot up in agitation. 'Are we going to confront her?' She searched Bryn's brilliant dark eyes. 'What if you're wrong?'

'I'm not wrong, Francey,' he told her bluntly. 'I've spoken at length to my grandmother about Gulla Nolan. There's a tie-up here. She and I have never had this discussion before, but I guessed that towards the end my grandfather had come to believe Sir Francis had played a part in Gulla's disappearance. My grandmother said—and this stunned me—Gulla had once saved her from Frank's highly unwelcome advances. Apparently he'd always had a thing for my grandmother, since before my grandparents were married and they were all friends. Gulla threatened to shoot Frank on the spot. Just imagine it! He meant it too. Frank would never have forgotten. It was his way to get square. It's Carina's way as well. She's always wanted to get square with you. Did you tell her we were engaged?'

'No, no—of course not.' Her emotions were in tumult. 'I've told no one. We announce it together, as planned.'

'We announce it to Carina *tonight*,' Bryn told her. 'Or rather *you* announce it. Be wearing your ring. I'll be behind the scenes. You won't tell her I'm here until we're ready to confront her. By the way, Bormann has gone missing. Big surprise! He was part of the plot. He would have to have made contingency plans. We know about Valerie Scott's part in things. I intend to string it all together for dear Carrie.'

'This is a nightmare.' Francesca groaned. 'I couldn't face it without you, Bryn.'

'You're not without me. We're together.' Bryn kissed her hard.

His rage at Carina and her actions would never in a million years drain away. She really shouldn't be allowed to go free. She deserved jail. But the scandal! Francesca would hate that.

'The best way to get rid of a nightmare like Carina is to banish her somewhere she can't ever seek to harm you again,' he said forcefully. 'She's always loved Monte Carlo, hasn't she? All the money and glamour. She can take up residence there. We can't have a huge scandal. The smartest thing Carina can do is transplant herself to the other side of the world. It's just big enough. She has the money. She's in no position to fight us.'

Francesca lifted her head to stare into his masterful face. 'This is shocking, Bryn. The most obscene thing possible. Annette could have been killed.'

'Don't!' A shudder passed directly from him into her. Fears for the two of them—his mother and the woman he so desperately loved—hadn't yet subsided.

'I think I know where Gulla's remains are,' she said gently.

'Francey!' He sat there stunned, and more than a little spooked. She'd said it as if it was fact.

'When this is over I'll show you, as Gulla showed me. His people will want to give him a ceremonial burial.'

Urgently he pulled her across his knees, burying his face in her neck. 'Oh, God, Francey, you're the best, the bravest, the most beautiful woman in all the world.'

'And a little crazy?' For the first time that evening she smiled.

'Never! You're protected by the Light.'

It was something that would draw people to her all her life, Bryn thought, but it was only for him, her future husband, to bask in its flame. Carina was the one who was crazy. The time had come for her to be held responsible—at least in part—for her actions.

EPILOGUE

LADY MACALLAN had insisted on giving the official engagement party. The news had swept the city, causing widespread coverage, a deluge of congratulations, expressions of delight and a good many hastily-got-together gala parties.

The general opinion was that this was the best possible outcome for the Macallan-Forsyth clans. Not only that, the best possible outcome for the city and for the giant state of Western Australia. Many benefits would flow from the union between these two very powerful families.

It wasn't all that much of a surprise for the city to learn that Carina Forsyth had decided to quit 'the backwater of Perth' for the glamour and culture of Europe. If more than a few people responded with 'good riddance', Carina was not to hear it. She had lost no time quitting the country of her birth, with a cold and haughty, 'I don't expect to return.' She would, however, in the fullness of time, marry a bogus Italian prince…

The beautiful one-shouldered gown Francesca had chosen for her engagement party, a one-of-a-kind silk-satin in a vibrant shade of cerise, couldn't have been more perfect for such an occasion—nor more perfect as a showcase for her very slender, supple body When she arrived with Bryn at the great, graceful Macallan mansion blazing with joy and pride, Lady Macallan took her aside to pin an heirloom sunburst of diamonds high on the gown's shoulder.

'It's gorgeous!' Francesca breathed, consumed with gratitude. She stared at her glowing reflection in the tall gilded mirror. 'I love it.'

'It looks wonderful on you!' Lady Macallan exclaimed, her beautifully coiffed head tipped to one side. 'And I think I always knew the girl I was going to pin it on.' She smiled. 'Welcome to the family, Francey.' Lightly she kissed Francesca's cheek. 'I couldn't be more happy for you and for Bryn. I adore my grandson. He is the light of my life. And I know he has loved you literally from childhood. Annette and I both knew. What I hadn't counted on was Annette finding a new love to fill *her* days,' she said with a chuckle. 'I expect she and Gordon will be married next, but I insist it's you and Bryn first.'

And that was exactly how it happened.

Charles Forsyth, happily reconciled with his wife, gave his beautiful niece away.

In front of the altar, with the Archbishop waiting to conduct the ceremony, the bride, exquisite in her bridal gown, a bouquet of white roses in her hand, her smile radiant, and the groom, in his finery a fitting match for his glorious bride, looked at one another with perfect understanding. Their love and happiness was so great it overflowed. It surged down the aisle and along the lavishly be-ribboned pews, so that the entire congregation was bathed in it, absorbing its wonderful glow.

Everything was absolutely *perfect.* Francesca even fancied she saw a shining vision of her parents. They were smiling at her, waving in silent valediction, before merging with the blaze of bejewelled light that poured through the cathedral's stained glass windows. Knowing herself blessed, Francesca turned her head to smile radiantly into the face of her soon-to-be husband.

His soul so beautifully complemented her own.

Love was the elusive key that opened up the door to an earthly happiness that made life complete.

MILLS & BOON PUBLISH EIGHT LARGE PRINT TITLES A MONTH. THESE ARE THE EIGHT TITLES FOR OCTOBER 2009.

MILLS & BOON PUBLISH EIGHT LARGE PRINT TITLES A MONTH. THESE ARE THE EIGHT TITLES FOR NOVEMBER 2009.

—————————— ❦ ——————————

THE GREEK TYCOON'S BLACKMAILED MISTRESS
Lynne Graham

RUTHLESS BILLIONAIRE, FORBIDDEN BABY
Emma Darcy

CONSTANTINE'S DEFIANT MISTRESS
Sharon Kendrick

THE SHEIKH'S LOVE-CHILD
Kate Hewitt

THE BROODING FRENCHMAN'S PROPOSAL
Rebecca Winters

HIS L.A. CINDERELLA
Trish Wylie

DATING THE REBEL TYCOON
Ally Blake

HER BABY WISH
Patricia Thayer

MILLS & BOON

millsandboon.co.uk Community

Join Us!

The Community is the perfect place to meet and chat to kindred spirits who love books and reading as much as you do, but it's also the place to:

- **Get the inside scoop from authors about their latest books**
- **Learn how to write a romance book with advice from our editors**
- **Help us to continue publishing the best in women's fiction**
- **Share your thoughts on the books we publish**
- **Befriend other users**

Forums: Interact with each other as well as authors, editors and a whole host of other users worldwide.

Blogs: Every registered community member has their own blog to tell the world what they're up to and what's on their mind.

Book Challenge: We're aiming to read 5,000 books and have joined forces with The Reading Agency in our inaugural Book Challenge.

Profile Page: Showcase yourself and keep a record of your recent community activity.

Social Networking: We've added buttons at the end of every post to share via digg, Facebook, Google, Yahoo, technorati and de.licio.us.

www.millsandboon.co.uk